because of
mr. terupt

because of mr. terupt

ROB BUYEA

delacorte press

Credit is extended to Marilyn Burns, creator of the dollar-words problem, and to Catherine Little, for her article on counting blades of grass in the September 1999 issue of the journal *Mathematics Teaching in the Middle School.*

Copyright © 2010 by Rob Buyea

All rights reserved. Published in the United States by Delacorte Press, an imprint of Random House Children's Books, a division of Random House, Inc., New York.

Delacorte Press is a registered trademark and the colophon is a trademark of Random House, Inc.

Library of Congress Cataloging-in-Publication Data
Buyea, Rob.
Because of Mr. Terupt / Rob Buyea. — 1st ed.
p. cm.
Summary: Seven fifth-graders at Snow Hill School in Connecticut relate how their lives are changed for the better by "rookie teacher" Mr. Terupt.
ISBN 978-0-385-73882-8 (hc : alk. paper) —
ISBN 978-0-375-89615-6 (ebook) — ISBN 978-0-385-90749-1
(glb : alk. paper) [1. Interpersonal relations—Fiction. 2. Teachers—Fiction. 3. Schools—Fiction. 3. Family life—Connecticut—Fiction. 5. Connecticut—Fiction.] I. Title.
PZ7.B98316Bec 2010
[Fic]—dc22
2010003414
The text of this book is set in 12-point Goudy.
Book design by Kenny Holcomb
Printed in the United States of America
10 9 8 7 6 5 4 3 2 1
First Edition

For the third and fourth graders at Bethany Community School, who inspired me to write, and whose everyday mysteries and spontaneity gave me a story to tell

 FOREWORD

I was no child when I first read and admired this instantly engaging first novel, which was once called (more seriously) *Voices from the Classroom* and then became (more whimsically) *The Dollar-Word Man*; at the time, I was finishing my twelfth novel. I'd already passed my midsixties when I saw Rob Buyea's excellent book grow and emerge as *Because of Mr. Terupt*—a more fitting title for a story about a life-changing teacher, one we all wish we had (and some of us *did*).

As for the children who tell us about Mr. Terupt, they are no less authentic than their magical teacher; they will remind you of your own friends and enemies. Even the accident toward which this novel is inevitably headed is no accident; it is as masterfully set up and skillfully concealed as the rest of this riveting story.

—John Irving

part one

september

Peter

It's our bad luck to have teachers in this world, but since we're stuck with them, the best we can do is hope to get a brand-new one instead of a mean old fart. New teachers don't know the rules, so you can get away with things the old-timers would squash you for. That was my theory. So I was feeling pretty excited to start fifth grade, since I was getting a rookie teacher—a guy named Mr. Terupt. Right away, I put him to the test.

If the bathroom pass is free, all you have to do is take it and go. This year, the bathrooms were right across the hall. It's always been an easy way to get out of doing work. I can be really sneaky like that. I take the pass all the time and the teachers never notice. And like I said, Mr. Terupt was a rookie, so I knew he wasn't going to catch me.

Once you're in the bathroom, it's mess-around time. All the other teachers on our floor were women, so you didn't have to worry about them barging in on you. Grab the bars to the stalls and swing. Try to touch your feet to the ceiling. Swing hard. If someone's in the stall, it's really funny to swing and kick his door in, especially if he's a younger kid. If you scare him bad enough, he might pee on himself a little. That's funny. Or if your buddy's using the urinal, you can push him from behind and flush it at the same time. Then he might get a little wet. That's pretty funny, too. Some kids like to plug the toilets with big wads of toilet paper, but I don't suggest you try doing that. You can get in big trouble. My older brother told me his friend got caught and he had to scrub the toilets with a toothbrush. He said the principal made him brush his teeth with that toothbrush afterward, too. Mrs. Williams is pretty tough, but I don't think she'd give out that kind of punishment. I don't want to find out, either.

When I came back into the classroom after my fourth or fifth trip, Mr. Terupt looked at me and said, "Boy, Peter, I'm gonna have to call you Mr. Peebody, or better yet, Peter the Pee-er. You do more peein' than a dog walking by a mile of fire hydrants."

Everybody laughed. I was wrong. He had noticed. I sat down. Then Mr. Terupt came over and whispered in my ear, "My grandpa used to tell me to tie a knot in it."

I didn't know what to do. My eyes got real big when he said that. I couldn't believe it. But that didn't matter. Mr. Terupt just went back to the front board and the math problem he was going over. I sat there with my big eyes. Soon a smile, too.

"What did he say?" Marty asked. Marty's desk was right next to mine.

"Nothing," I said.

Ben and Wendy leaned across their desks to hear. They sat right across from us. Our four desks made up table number three. Mr. Terupt called us by tables sometimes.

"Nothing," I said again. It would be my secret.

How cool was Mr. Terupt? His reaction was better than being yelled at like the old farts would have done. Some kids in my class would have cried, but not me. And somehow, I think Mr. Terupt knew I wouldn't. It was his way of letting me know he knew what was going on without making a huge stink about it. I liked that about Mr. Terupt. He sure could be funny. And I'm a funny guy. This year, for the first time in my life, I started thinking school could be fun.

Jessica

Act 1, Scene 1

The first day of school. I was nervous. Somewhat. The sweaty-palms-and-dry-mouth syndrome struck. This wasn't surprising—after all, I was coming to a brand-new place. My mom and I had just moved all the way from the Pacific Ocean to the Atlantic Ocean, over here in Connecticut. So it was my first, first day in Snow Hill School. My mom came to help me get settled.

We walked through the glass doors and beautiful entry-way and stopped in the main office to ask for directions. A red-haired woman who proved to be exceptional at multi-tasking greeted us with a smile and a slight nod. She did this while the phone rested between her ear and shoulder, allowing her hands to scribble notes from a conversation she was having in her free ear with the brown-haired lady standing next to her. We waited. My fingers dug into the hard cover of my book.

"Hi. I'm Mrs. Williams, the principal." This was the brown-haired lady speaking. She looked serious, all decked out in her business suit. "Welcome to Snow Hill School. Can I help you with anything?"

"We're looking for Mr. Terupt's room," Mom said. "I'm Julie Writeman and this is my daughter, Jessica. We're new in town."

"Ah, yes. It's a pleasure to meet you both. Let me show you the way."

Mrs. Williams led us out of the office. I glanced at the secretary one more time. She'd be a great character in one of Dad's plays, I thought. My dad directs small plays in California, where I still wanted to be.

"How are you today, Jessica?" Mrs. Williams asked.

"Fine," I said, although that wasn't really true.

We followed Mrs. Williams across the lobby and upstairs in search of my new fifth-grade classroom. The halls smelled stuffy but clean, like they'd just been disinfected. I wondered if the custodians had done that on purpose, to make a show of how clean their school was. I followed Mom down the blue-speckled carpet and past the rows of red lockers, where some kids were already unloading new supplies. I could feel all their eyes studying the new girl in town. After the stares came the whispers. My face burned.

"Here you are," Mrs. Williams said. "This is your floor. There are four classrooms up here, all fifth grade, two on each side of the hall with the bathrooms right in the middle." Mrs. Williams pointed as she spoke. "That's your classroom." She pointed again. "Room two-oh-two. Have a good first day."

"Thank you," Mom said. I just nodded.

Act 1, Scene 2

We walked into the classroom. The teacher looked up from his desk and smiled at us. The butterflies in my stomach fluttered as if I were on a Tilt-A-Whirl.

"Good morning. I'm Mr. Terupt," the teacher said as Mom and I walked in. He came right over to greet us.

"Good morning," Mom said back. "I'm Julie Writeman, and this is Jessica. I think she's a little nervous being a new student."

My tongue felt so swollen that I couldn't talk. I settled on returning Mr. Terupt's smile. It was a friendly one.

"Well, this is my first day, too. So I guess we'll try to figure things out together," he said.

My smile grew.

"Your seat is right over there at table two. You're with Natalie, Tommy, and Ryan. Being near the windows should give you some good reading light. That's a great book you have there, Jessica."

I looked down at my book, A Wrinkle in Time. I rubbed my hand over the cover.

"I really like happy endings," I said.

"Me too," Mr. Terupt said. "I'll do my best to give you a happy ending this year."

I smiled again. I couldn't believe it. My teacher was new, too. And he liked what I was reading. I don't know why, but somehow he made my butterflies disappear and my tongue shrink. Things were going to be okay.

LUKE

I like school. I'm good at it. I get all As. So when Mr. Terupt announced our first math project, I was excited.

Dollar Words was crazy. Definitely not a worksheet problem, like all the others I've ever been given. Not even close! We had to assume that the letter *a* was worth one cent, *b* two cents, *c* three cents—and so on, making the letter *z* worth twenty-six cents. The challenge was to find words that equaled one dollar when you added up their letter values. Not ninety-nine cents or a dollar and one cent, but one dollar exactly.

Mr. Terupt gave us time to get started. He wanted to make sure we understood the project, and he said he wondered who would be the first one to find a dollar word.

I immediately made a data table of all the letters and their corresponding values. A quick reference for me. Then I started putting down any word that came to mind that had some of the bigger letters in it. *Pretty* = 104. *Walnut* = 91. *Mister* = 84. Then I thought, Hey, wait a minute, what if I just tack on the letter *s*? *Misters* = 103. No good, but very close. I figured this could still be a worthwhile strategy for other words.

So there I was cranking out words, trying to find the first dollar word of the year, when what do I hear? Peter and Alexia.

This is the fourth year Peter's been in my class, and my third time with Alexia. Peter's funny, but sometimes he gets to be too much. If I'm concentrating on my work and he just wants to joke around, it annoys me. But I like him. He's fun, and he's no stranger to trouble. Alexia, on the other hand, is always involved in some "girl war." That stuff I don't get. She loves to wear flashy clothes—dresses, skirts, fancy shoes—and she always has the accessories to go with them. And she says the word *like* way too much. Alexia isn't a stranger to trouble, either. She and Peter are a good match.

Peter elbowed Alexia. Then I heard him whisper a word to her.

That's not even close to a dollar, I thought.

"Fifty-three," Alexia said. "No good. Try . . ."

Were they crazy? They were trying out rude words and giggling the whole time. I just knew they were going to get caught.

"That's no good, either," Peter said. "Maybe . . ."

What a butthead! As soon as I thought it, I knew it was a word worth calculating. Sure enough, *butthead* equaled 81. I tacked on the *s*. There wasn't just one butthead but two *buttheads* (dollar word). I was just about to call out that I had found one when Peter beat me to it.

"I've got a word!" he yelled. "*Buttocks!*" He strutted to the board like he was the coolest thing since sliced bread and wrote it for the class. "*Buttocks*," he said again. "B-U-T-T-O-C-S." Peter went on to demonstrate how the word added up to a dollar. Mr. Terupt didn't interrupt. Just as I was about to, the new girl did.

"*Buttocks* is spelled with a *k* in it, Peter," Jessica said.

Peter looked to Mr. Terupt. "Sorry, Peter. She's right. Better try again. And maybe you should choose a different type of word than the ones you've been coming up with."

Peter slunk back to his seat. No surprise to me, Mr. Terupt knew what Peter was up to the whole time.

I raised my hand. "Mr. Terupt, I've got one." I walked up to the board and wrote *butthead*. That was followed by a chorus of laughs. "*Butthead*," I said. "B-U-T-T-H-E-A-D adds up to eighty-one cents, but if we have more than one, then we get *buttheads*. And *buttheads* is a dollar word. Just ask Peter and Alexia."

Mr. Terupt snickered. "That's enough, Luke. I must say, this isn't a word I was expecting, but nonetheless, it's our first dollar word. Congratulations."

Dollar Words was the best math project ever. We started it on a *Wednesday* (dollar word) and worked for three weeks. Through trial and error, a few strategies that I learned along the way, and some helpful hints from Mr. Terupt, I broke the record for most dollar words. My final poster was covered with fifty-four of them.

Mr. Terupt looked at my work and smiled. "Luke, this is *excellent*." (Dollar word.) "You are the dollar-word champ."

Alexia

I was like, I have this new guy for a teacher. That's so cool.

Mr. Terupt was nice. He let us sit in tables, not rows. I was like, no way, are you serious? And like, the best was I got to sit with my friend Danielle.

There was this new girl in our class, Jessica. She wasn't at our table, but I needed to talk to her. I needed to tell her who she could be friends with. She seemed like she could be pretty cool, even though she carried a book around like a teddy bear.

I found her at recess. Outdoor recess is held behind the school. There's a big blacktop area with basketball hoops and hopscotch. There's playground equipment in another spot, and a large field for running around and playing sports, like kickball or football. That's where the gazebo is, too—by the edge of the field. I found Jessica sitting alone on the steps of the gazebo. She was reading a book. I was like, What a loser, but I went up to her.

"Hey," I said.

"Hi," she said back.

"You're Jessica, right?"

"Yes."

I blew a bubble with my gum and sat down. "I'm Alexia," I said. "My friends call me Lexie." I found the compact mirror in my purse and checked my Rock Star Purple lip gloss. Then I was like, "Where'd you come from?"

"We moved from California," the new girl said.

"I used to live in California, too." I started playing with the stones that lay under my feet. It's always been easier for me to lie when I don't have to look at the person's eyes. "We moved because, like, my dad got sick and needed the doctors here."

"I'm sorry," Jessica said. She started playing with the stones now, too.

"Listen," I said. "Like, you're new here so let me help you out a little . . . if you want, that is." I snapped my gum.

"Sure. Okay."

I stopped playing with the stones and scooted closer to her. "Want a piece of gum?"

"No thanks," she said.

Of course not. Little Miss Perfect. I put the gum back in my purse.

"That girl," I said, pointing to Danielle across the playground. "You can't miss her. She's the fat one." I laughed, but Jessica didn't. "That's Danielle. Watch out for her. She's, like, somebody you don't want to be friends with."

"But don't you sit with her in class? I thought you were friends."

I wasn't expecting this. Usually girls just listen and follow along. I blew a bubble and snapped my gum again. "Yeah. She used to be cool. But like, she's been saying stuff about you. Calling you Miss Goody Two-shoes and a snotty book-worm."

Jessica seemed surprised. "Oh. Okay. Thanks for letting me know," she said.

"Don't worry." I put my arm around her. "Stick with me and I'll, like, help you out. It'll be great."

Then recess ended. That's how I got the girl war started.

Jeffrey

The kids in my class are all right. I have to deal with Alexia again. Plus her feather boas and leopard-print clothes and her stupid purse. I wonder what kind of makeup she puts on this year. She's so dumb. She thinks she's a Hollywood star or somethin'.

Then there's Luke. I don't mind him. He's just smart and serious about school.

And Danielle's in my class. She's fat.

And then there's Peter. A wise guy. A total smart aleck. I wanted to tell Terupt that Peter spent all his time in the bathroom 'cause he was messin' around.

But Terupt figured it out, even if he was new. He seems smart. I just don't want him tryin' to figure me out. I'm no good in school. School sucks.

Danielle

School wasn't so great. My teacher seemed pretty nice, and he could be funny, too, but none of that matters when you don't have friends. Lexie had done this stuff to me before. One day she's my friend, the next she's not. I don't even know why. I'm not mean to her. This year was the worst, though.

Things started out fine. Then one day after recess, Lexie started ignoring me. Pretending I wasn't there. She would talk about things right in front of me and leave me out of the conversation. She started telling her stupid fat jokes. It was horrible. I cried at home a lot.

I'm a little heavy—well, bigger, I guess. I don't like saying I'm fat. I don't know why I am. I watch what I eat and I don't have any more than the other girls at lunch. Mom says I'll grow into my body. She's not fat. Neither is my brother Charlie, or Grandma, or Grandpa, or Dad. Grandma says, "You've got to have some meat on your bones, girl." Yeah, Grandma, I think—so someone like Lexie can tell fat jokes about me. I don't say anything, though. Grandma doesn't get it. Only Mom understands, and I feel a little better when she reassures me that I'll thin out as I grow. She also tells me that there must be a reason I'm having to deal with this. "It's making you a better person," she says, "and someday this experience will help you." That's all great, but I wish I could grow into my body now.

We live on a farm. My mom grew up here. My grandma and grandpa live in their own house next to ours. They help us run the farm. So my grandma's around a lot, and she wanted to know what was wrong with me—why I was crying.

Any time I mentioned Lexie she'd get all mad: "I'm goin' into that school and fix that girl," she'd say.

"No, Grandma."

"Why are you even still friends with her? She doesn't know how to treat people well, specially a friend."

"It's not her fault, Grandma. It's this new girl's fault," I said, sticking up for Lexie the way I always do. "A new girl that I can't stand."

"If you keep telling yourself that, it won't ever get better," Grandma said. She's a tough woman.

The only time I've got friends is when I'm in Lexie's group. Nobody wants to be friends with the fat kid. I don't know what to do.

Grandma said a prayer with me that night. We knelt by my bed.

ANNA

I didn't say much in school, and I never raised my hand. That would have been an easy way for people to notice me, and I didn't want to be noticed. People can be real mean. That's something Mom warned me about. And my mom knows, trust me. I didn't have any close friends and I wasn't looking for any. Mom was my best friend.

Not getting noticed was never a problem for me before. I was always quiet and I behaved, so the teachers left me alone. I kept my head down and looked at the floor a lot. But I'm a good observer. Mrs. Williams, our principal, winks whenever there's some big surprise coming. It's something I noticed a few years ago. If you keep quiet, you have time to look and listen and take things in.

At the beginning of the year, the first thing you pay attention to is the classroom. We had a nice room. A big one. There was a whole wall of windows opposite the door. Mr. Terupt's desk was in the corner by those windows. The students' desks were arranged in five tables of four. So right away I knew we had a teacher who was into teamwork and who probably didn't mind a little talking—otherwise, we would have been in old-fashioned rows. The front of the room had the blackboard and the back wall had a whiteboard. The last side of the room had all our cabinets and a sink, plus a drinking fountain. Most of the room was carpeted, except for the side by the sink and fountain. Our door was next to the fountain.

The other thing—the bigger thing you pay attention to, in the beginning—is your teacher, especially if he's new like Mr. Terupt. Right away, I could tell that he was a reader, because there were books everywhere in our room. Mom liked that when I told her. Mom's a library assistant in another school. It's a good job. She has the same schedule I do, and it allows her to take some classes at night. She's studying art, something she missed out on when she was younger. She's really good at drawing and painting.

Mr. Terupt was young and athletic-looking. He didn't have any pictures around his desk, and he didn't wear a wedding ring. Ms. Newberry, from across the hall, didn't have a wedding ring, either. Neither did Mom.

Mr. Terupt turned out to be different. He noticed me on the first day. It didn't matter that I wasn't raising my hand because he would say, "Anna, get ready. I'm calling on you next." Or if we were talking about something and there wasn't just one opinion, he would say, "Anna, what do you think?"

He wasn't going to let me hide all year. This made me nervous, but it turned out to be a good thing in the end.

october

Peter

I never ever had something in school excite me before, but the plant unit we did with Mr. T had me fired up. We grew these bean plants from seeds, and—once they got big enough—we started doing different tests with them. Variables, Mr. T called them. First we stuffed the plants in boxes, with just a little tiny hole in the side, and we waited to see what the plants would do after a few days in the dark.

Anna had a meltdown about it. "I don't want to put mine in a box!" she cried. Mr. T had to take her out in the hall to calm her down. I was kind of shocked. Usually she doesn't say anything. What a weirdo, I thought. It's no wonder she doesn't have any friends. It's a good thing Danielle was her partner. She's the patient kind. Anyone else would have been

fuming. My partner was Lexie, which was fine. She let me do what I wanted.

Next we put the plants on their side to see how they would grow. I couldn't believe it. The plants bent and still grew up toward the ceiling. That was pretty cool. But the best part was what we got to do in the end.

Mr. T let us feed our plant any concoction we wanted to over the course of a week. There was just one rule: We couldn't use an ingredient that would spoil and stink up the classroom, like milk, or something that wasn't good for us to breathe, like gas.

There were some pretty wild concoctions. David and Nick used salad dressing because according to them, "Plants make salad, so the plant will like salad dressing." Brenda and Heather used orange juice mixed with ketchup and Pepto-Bismol. I don't know what they were thinking. Mine was the best, though.

I brought in cat litter (used), soda, and a little maple syrup. I did my best to mix it together and feed it to my plant. Lexie wasn't real happy about my choice of ingredients. I didn't tell her I had peed in my soda bottle some, too.

"Peter, you moron. This stuff is gonna kill our plant," she whined.

"Shut up. You never cared about the plant before," I said.

"Well, I care now," she said.

"Lexie. Maple syrup comes from trees. I drink soda a lot, and I'm growing—and farmers put animal manure on their fields all the time. So zip it. It's going to work."

Our plant was dead in two days.

Danielle and Anna did the best. Danielle used some

natural ingredients her grandmother had taught her about. Something the old-time farmers really did use, I guess. Danielle lives on a farm, so she had a big advantage. Her concoction worked. Big-time! She and Anna were the only ones to come up with food that the plant liked.

Anna was all smiles until Lexie said, "Like, you're just lucky Danielle was your partner. She did everything." Then Lexie turned to me and added, "Even if she is fat." I don't think anyone else heard, but I laughed. I know I probably shouldn't have. Anna's smile disappeared, and she stared at the floor.

Poor old Luke sure tried. I think he put too much brainpower in it. And he's got a lot of brainpower. He's been the smartest kid in school since kindergarten. His partner was Jeffrey, but he never does anything. He just let Luke take charge. Maybe he should have helped.

"I've brought in a number of different ingredients," Luke said, "and they'll interact perfectly because of the electron balance and resulting bond formations." He even said something about a periodic table, or some crazy thing.

Well, you're never going to believe this, but Luke mixed his junk together and it started smoking. The next thing we knew, the stupid fire alarm was going off. The whole school had to go outside and even the fire department showed up. It was great!

Mr. T had to do some explaining, and after a while we were let back inside, but Luke wasn't performing any more experiments for us.

Man, things were just so much fun with Mr. T.

LUKE

We moved from cool math right into wicked science. The only thing I didn't like about our science unit was that we had to have partners. I prefer to do my projects alone, but Mr. Terupt teamed us up. We were working with plants and he said we didn't have enough space for everyone to have their own. Jeffrey was my partner, which—believe it or not—worked out great because he let me do whatever I wanted. He didn't care. The only bad part was that he was always *grumpy* (dollar word).

We studied phototropisms by observing how our plant grew toward light after we stuffed it into a box that had only a tiny hole in its side. Then we studied geotropism by observing how our plant grew toward the ceiling, even after we tipped the plant on its side for a few days. And then we were given the opportunity to study a variable on our own.

Mr. Terupt told us to manipulate the plant's nourishment. "Feed it whatever you want," he said. "Make your own concoctions."

Jeffrey left me alone. He hated school and everything about it.

That day I hurried home and studied my periodic table. I had received a special chemistry set last Christmas. Hydrogen and oxygen make a special bond when they come together to form water, so I figured I should try to recreate that special bond with whatever *molecular* (dollar word) ingredients I chose. I looked through the chemicals in my set and picked the ones that would result in the same type of electron balance that occurred in the hydrogen-and-oxygen bond.

I took my ingredients to school and got ready to measure and mix. Jeffrey was slightly interested at this point. Mr. Terupt, on the other hand, appeared a little uneasy about the whole thing, but he never stopped me.

"Luke, sometimes when you mix chemicals it can cause a reaction, which then *explodes* (dollar word)."

"I know," I said.

"Maybe we shouldn't mix these in the classroom without knowing what's going to happen," he said. "It might not be safe."

"All these potions came from my chemistry set at home. My mom saw it. It's safe," I said, trying my best to convince

Mr. Terupt. I didn't tell Mom or Mr. Terupt about the few ingredients I got from Dad's garage. I knew it would work.

"Hey, guys, come and look at all the stuff Luke's mixing together," Chris yelled.

I felt everyone gather behind me as I began mixing my substances together in a bowl, but before I could feed my plant, something happened. First the bowl started feeling warmer—then hot. The potion turned dark green—then gray. It started bubbling—first slowly, then rapidly. I knew this was bad.

"Back up! Everybody back up! Get away from it!" Mr. Terupt ordered.

Smoke started billowing from my concoction. Then the screech of the fire alarm pounded against my ears. The only other thing I heard was Peter laughing. "This is awesome!" he yelled. "Way to go, Lukester!"

"Outside! Everybody outside!" Mr. Terupt ordered.

I was done for. I was sure of it.

Wrong again.

Mr. Terupt spoke to Mrs. Williams and took the blame for everything. He even stood up to the fire marshal, who always walks through the building after an unannounced fire alarm. The marshal wanted our dollar-word posters taken off the hallway walls. He claimed they were a fire hazard. Jeffrey thought this confrontation was a big deal.

"Did you see Terupt say no to that guy?" he said. "He refused to take our posters down."

"I saw," I said. And I saw flashbacks of smoke pouring out of the bowl. I knew I wasn't ever going to be a *botanist* (dollar word).

At least Jeffrey had gotten excited about something.

I wish Mr. Terupt hadn't trusted us so much. Maybe it was because he was a first-year teacher and didn't know better. But I don't think that was it. I think it was a case of Mr. Terupt being a special teacher.

Jeffrey

Luke was tryin' to feed our plant. I saw the smoke risin'. I knew what was gonna happen. Terupt did, too, 'cause I saw him go to the windows right away. Not fast enough, though. The alarm still went off. The whole school had to go outside 'cause of Luke.

When we came back in, some guy was walkin' down the hall with our janitors, Mr. Lumas and Mr. Ruddy. Terupt sent us into the classroom, but he stayed in the hall. I hid by the door to listen.

"All of it!" the man yelled. "I want all of it off the walls!" He was pointing at our math posters.

Mr. Lumas looked at Terupt. "You heard him," he said.

"I'm not taking them down," Terupt said.

"Do you know who this is?" Mr. Ruddy said. "This is the fire marshal."

Terupt said, "I don't care who it is. I'm not taking them down." He looked at the fire marshal and said, "You have no idea how hard my kids worked on these."

He was pointing at our posters. He was pointing at my poster. It had one word on it, *stupid*, and it wasn't even a dollar word. All of a sudden I felt bad 'cause I hadn't tried on Terupt's project.

There were some more words said, but then the fire marshal left. The posters stayed. I hope he felt stupid.

Terupt came back into the room. Peter was out of his seat. "Mr. T, you just told that guy off," Peter said, dancing around. "That was awesome!"

"No, I didn't," Terupt said. "Get in your seat. You shouldn't have seen that."

But I saw it, and I heard it. Terupt stuck up for us. There's always posters up in the school halls, and they're never fire hazards. I think the fire marshal was just mad about our false alarm, and I think Terupt knew that, too. He wasn't gonna get pushed around. Our hard work mattered to Terupt—even mine. I owed him now. I had to try, even if only a little.

anna

I didn't want my plant to die. I didn't want to put it in the box. Everybody was staring at me. I started crying.

Mr. Terupt took me out into the hall. "Anna, what's wrong?"

"I don't want to kill my plant," I blurted out. My back slid down the wall and I put my head in my hands.

"We're not going to kill your plant." Mr. Terupt knelt down in front of me.

"Yes, you are," I said. "If we put it in the box, it's going to kill it."

"We'll take it out before it dies," he promised.

"No. I don't want to hurt it."

"Tell you what, Anna. Let's do the experiments that are

lined up for your plant. We have to, because Danielle is your partner and she needs to do the science, too. Then, when we're all done, I'll let you take *my* plant. Our control. The one we don't do anything to."

I still didn't like the idea of hurting my plant, but I liked the idea of getting the control. I think he saw my hesitation.

"Plus, since you're working with Danielle, I have a feeling that your plant is actually going to be just fine."

I don't know Danielle that well. She's never been in my class before. She seems nice. I like her. Sometimes she's friends with Alexia. I don't know why. I'm glad I'm partners with Danielle and not Alexia. I've never been in Alexia's class, but I can tell she's mean. All the girls listen to her, though. Katie, Emily, Heather, Natalie—all of them. Not me. I stay away from her.

My mom has warned me not to get involved in that popularity stuff. She was ostracized once. That means nobody wanted to be friends with her. My mom told me it was like there was a big group of people holding hands in a circle, and she was never let in. She always had to stand outside the circle. Mom doesn't ever want that to happen to me. It was when she was sixteen and pregnant with me. I can tell that she still hurts inside from all of it. Even her own parents shunned her. That's why she quit school shortly after I was born, and moved out. She tried to move in with my dad (I've never met him), but that didn't work out—he left. Mom says we can talk about my dad and the whole situation when I'm older. All I know is that she says he's a nice man. My grandma and grandpa (I've never met them, either) still don't want anything to do with us. They moved far away after my mom moved out. My mom might be young, but she's still a great mom. She's my best friend, and I love her. If you love someone, you don't quit on them just because they make a mistake.

Mr. Terupt helped me stand up. "Trust me on this one," he said. "Be positive."

We headed back into the classroom. My plant went into the box and came out a few days later, a little yellow and without a lot of new growth. But it was alive! Turning it on its side wasn't harmful, so I was okay with that test, and then it was our chance to feed it whatever we wanted.

Mr. Terupt was right. Danielle knew what she was doing. "Here's a list of things we could mix together," Danielle said.

I read the list. I didn't know everything on it. How did she?

"My grandmother helped me with it," she said. "She's always been good at growing things. She's the reason we have successful crops on the farm."

Both of us brought in some of the ingredients. We mixed them together and fed our plant. Ours was the only one to survive! It turned really green, and grew and grew and grew.

I took the control home, but Danielle and I decided to leave our plant in school. We kept feeding it and everyone watched it grow. It grew almost to the ceiling, wrapping itself around the cord to the blinds, all the way up. Then one day it was knocked over. Somehow our super-duper plant fell off the windowsill. Nobody knows how it happened. I have a pretty good idea, though. I bet Alexia did it, because it happened when she was being nasty to Danielle. I'm thankful that Mr. Terupt let me take the control home. I didn't want her to hurt that one, too.

I liked being Danielle's partner. I wonder now if Mr. Terupt knew what he was starting between me and Danielle. I wonder.

Jessica

Act 2, Scene 1

My daily routine included lunch with Alexia and the girls, minus Danielle and Anna—they sat alone—and then recess. Alexia found it funny to see how upset Danielle would get.

Right about this same time, I was finishing the book *Belle Teal*. I loved Belle. I wanted her to be my friend. She was honest and courageous. What would Belle do in my shoes? That was easy. She would do the right thing. And doing the right thing meant giving someone a chance. Danielle didn't seem anything like Alexia made her out to be. I decided it was time to talk to Danielle and find out for myself.

Act 2, Scene 2

I set out to find Danielle the next day at recess. I spotted her from a distance. She was drawing in the dirt with a stick.

"Hi, Danielle," I said as I approached, clutching my latest book, *Where the Red Fern Grows*, close to me.

"What do you want?" she shot back, jabbing her stick too hard into the ground, causing it to snap in half. She turned away. It sounded like she was crying.

"Are you okay?" I walked closer.

"No. Lexie's being really mean to me, and it's all your fault!" She threw her sticks onto the ground.

My fault? She blamed me? Why didn't I see it coming? It made perfect sense: I was the new girl, and my arrival pushed her out of the group.

"I'm sorry," I said. I stood there. I wanted to be back in California, anyway. I missed my dad.

Danielle began scratching pictures in the dirt with her finger. "I'm sorry I said that. It's not your fault."

I sat down.

"It's just that Lexie's ignoring me—talking about me, saying mean stuff," Danielle went on. "She doesn't sit with me at lunch. She's not playing with me. And now all the other girls are doing the same thing. They always do what Alexia says. Anna's the only one who's still nice, and I'm not supposed to be friends with her."

"Why not?" I asked.

"My family, especially my grandma, think she's a bad influence."

"I don't get it."

"My mom and dad used to be friends with her grand-parents and—"

"You mean her parents," I interrupted.

"No, her grandparents." Danielle stopped moving the dirt and sat up to explain. "My mom and dad are forty-seven. They had my older brother, Charlie, when they were twenty—the same time Anna's grandparents had Anna's mother. They were all friends at church, that's how they knew each other. Charlie is twenty-seven, so Anna's mom must be twenty-seven, too."

"And Anna's eleven," I said, quickly putting all the pieces together. "So that means her mom was sixteen when Anna was born."

"That's right," Danielle said.

"And that's why your family, especially your grand-mother, thinks Anna will be a bad influence?" I asked.

"Yes," Danielle said. "I think they figure Anna will be like her mother, and that's not the type of people church-goers should associate with."

I didn't like what I was hearing. None of it seemed fair to Anna, but I wanted to learn more about her mother's story. "What happened after Anna was born?"

"I'm not sure," Danielle said. "I just know that it's only Anna and her mother now."

"None of that's her fault," I said matter-of-factly.

Danielle nodded. She bent forward and started drawing in the dirt again. I decided not to push it any more. She seemed upset by it, too.

"I'll play with you," I said.

"You will?" The hint of a smile spread its way across Danielle's dirt-streaked, teary face.

"Sure. And I won't listen to Alexia." I slid *Where the Red Fern Grows* off to the side and dug into the earth with my finger.

"I know that book. My grandma read it to me."

"It's very good," I said. "Everybody always likes a character with a dog. That's something my dad told me."

"It's a sad story," Danielle said, "but I won't tell you what happens."

"Please don't. We can talk about it when I get done, though."

"Sure," she said, shrugging her shoulders.

We sat next to each other scratching pictures in the dirt until the whistle sounded. Recess was over. We stood and brushed ourselves off. That was when I saw Danielle's dirt sketch of two dogs.

"That's a great picture, Danielle."

"Thanks," she said.

I liked Danielle. There were a lot of interesting things to learn about her, I could tell. I grabbed my book and we headed toward the building. Then I saw Anna wandering over by herself. I wondered if she wanted to be a loner. Or did she want friends? Why did she try so hard to be invisible? Was she embarrassed by her family situation? And how many people actually knew all that stuff about her mother?

Act 2, Scene 3

I was walking with Danielle when all of a sudden she rushed ahead and hurried inside. Looking up, I found out why. Alexia got right in my face.

"Like, whadaya doing? I thought I told you not to be friends with her." Alexia's head jerked from side to side as she talked. It reminded me of a bobblehead. She blocked my way, her hands on her cheetah-patterned hips.

"There's nothing wrong with Danielle. Besides, I can play with whomever I want," I said.

"Fine. Then like, you're not my friend anymore," Alexia said. She knocked *Where the Red Fern Grows* out of my hands. Then she whipped around and stomped inside.

I wasn't upset—but I'm not stupid, either. I knew Alexia was going to make my life miserable. That was her game. And she was good at it, too. Still, I had no clue how bad things would really get.

Alexia

I saw Jessica talking to Danielle. I saw them playing. That double-crossing, no-good Miss Perfect from California. She was gonna get it.

I went right up to her after recess and smacked her stupid book out of her hands. Who did she think she was, messing things up? I couldn't let her stand up to me and get away with it. Then somebody else might think they could do that, too. I wasn't about to let that happen. Nobody messes with Alexia.

Then I had to deal with Danielle. I caught up to her inside and followed her into the bathroom. I was like, "Whadaya doing?"

She backed up to the stall. "Nothing. What's wrong?"

I was like, "You're crazy to be friends with the new girl.

I told you she's been saying nasty stuff about you. How you smell like the farm. And just now she said, 'Who's bigger, Danielle or the cows?'"

Now Danielle was crying. Score! I hugged her. I was like, "We've been friends a long time, Danielle. Since second grade. We don't need her." She was still crying. I hugged her again. I was thinking, This will teach you to mess with me, Miss Perfect.

I let go of Danielle and walked over and stood in front of the mirror. I fixed the scrunchie in my hair and readjusted my scarf. I reapplied some Princess Pink lip gloss.

I was like, "Don't you worry, Danielle. We'll get her."

Danielle

I ended up talking and playing with Jessica at recess. My troubles with Lexie weren't her fault. I told Jessica about Anna. Jessica thought Anna seemed nice, which was true. Anna was my science partner for the plant unit, and I liked working with her.

"You stay away from that girl, you hear me?" Grandma said when I first mentioned Anna at home.

"Your grandmother's right, Danielle. That girl comes from a bad family," Mom said. "She'll be a bad influence."

I wanted to know why, so Grandma filled me in on Anna's family story. I just listened, but I couldn't help thinking about the Anna I knew. She didn't seem bad at all. In fact, I already liked her. I wanted her to be my friend.

I figured that as long as I wasn't going over to her house, I could be friends with Anna in school.

Before long it was time to head inside. I walked alongside Jessica until I saw Lexie marching toward us. She had a mean scowl on her face. She looked mad. Real mad—like a mama cow determined to keep you away from her new calf. I rushed ahead. I didn't want to fight. I felt bad for leaving Jessica behind, but I wanted to avoid Lexie. I hurried inside and hid in the bathroom, but Lexie found me.

The bathroom door flew open and she got right in my face. She told me all the mean things Jessica was saying about me.

"Like, you can even ask Katie or Emily. They'll tell ya. Little Miss California's a two-face. Nice to your face and mean behind it. You need to stay away from her."

I started crying. Why would Jessica say those mean things? Lexie hugged me for a second, but it didn't make me feel any better. Then she walked toward the sinks. She stood in front of the mirror fixing herself. I sat in one of the stalls, wiping my tears. "Like, ya know what else?" Lexie said. "Jessica's the one who killed your plant. Like, she knocked it over on purpose. She told me."

I've known Lexie since second grade, when she was all nice. She even came over to my house once that spring, but her feather boas weren't a good match for my farm, so she hasn't ever been back. And then in third grade, she started with her mean games, so I've never been to her house. We're friends in school, when Lexie says so, and that's it. Grandma says something's going on with Lexie that we don't know about, and that it's best not to worry about being her friend.

But I did worry. What was the truth? Was there anyone I could be friends with?

Dear God,

It's Danielle. I'm going to need your help sorting all this girl stuff out. I hope you don't mind. I'd rather not get Grandma involved. She doesn't always understand. Thanks. Amen.

november

LUKE

It was November. Apparently that meant time for Mr. Terupt to get crazy with his math ideas again. I think he was on a mission to put us through his math *gauntlet* (dollar word). "We're going to figure out the number of blades of grass in the soccer field," he announced one day.

"What! You're gonna make us count grass?" Peter yelled. "That's nuts!"

"No way!" Nick was *hollering* (dollar word).

"How are we supposed to do that?" Tommy said.

I raised my hand.

"Yes, Luke."

"You mean we're going to *estimate* the total number, right?" I said.

"Yes and no," Mr. Terupt said. "We'll actually do some calculating to get a reasonable approximation."

I was beginning to think that Peter might be right.

"Yes, it's going to be difficult, but I know we can do it," Mr. Terupt said. "Besides, if everything we did were easy, then you wouldn't learn anything. We need to be challenged in order to learn."

Mr. Terupt was right about it being a challenge. None of us had any idea how we were going to count blades of grass. But we did.

First we decided we wanted to count ten-centimeter-by-ten-centimeter squares, which was my suggestion after Mr. Terupt talked to us about sampling and how our government gets population numbers. Then we measured the squares on large pieces of cardboard and cut them out, so we were left with a piece of cardboard that had a ten-centimeter square missing in the middle. That was Mr. Terupt's suggestion. Now it would be easy to toss our piece of cardboard around the field and collect random ten-centimeter samples. So far so good. Time to head outside.

We marched downstairs and out the front doors by the office. Then we stampeded down the sidewalk until the end of the building. The soccer field awaited us on the side of our school.

Peter

She was bent over counting blades of grass. It was the perfect opportunity. Mr. T was busy helping someone else, so he wasn't going to see me in action.

I gripped the cardboard with my best hold, dipped my knees a little, and let the Frisbee fly. It zinged through the air on its mission like a missile from a fighter jet. Bull's-eye!

"Ow!" Lexie shrieked. "My tushie!"

I almost died of laughter. I dropped to my knees, I laughed so hard. I couldn't stop. I couldn't catch my breath, either. Lots of other kids were laughing, too.

Lexie yelled something about her "tushie" and me being a jerk. Everyone that missed out on the fun kept asking, "What happened? What happened?" Everyone except Mr. T.

He came right over to make sure Lexie wasn't injured.

Lexie was holding her "tushie" and hopping up and down, saying "Ow" over and over. She's a total drama queen. Usually a teacher checks the spot that hurts, but I don't think Mr. T was real big on that this time.

"Peter, that's not funny," Mr. T said to me. "Someone could have been injured. You're lucky you didn't hit anyone in the eye. Go sit down."

I sat down. It was no big deal. If you'd been there, you'd agree, it was superfunny.

LUKE

We spread out all over the place, tossing our cardboard squares and counting the blades of grass. Peter, however, was flinging his square like a Frisbee, even though Mr. Terupt had warned us that it wasn't a toy and to be careful throwing it.

Maybe if things had turned out differently that day, they would have turned out differently in the end, too. I think what happened on the soccer field just set us up for disaster later on.

So Peter was being his typical sneaky self, flinging his square and counting here and there. But as soon as he spotted Alexia bent over her square, he wound up and sailed a beauty in her direction. It was a perfect *delivery* (dollar word) that *tattooed* (dollar word) her fanny.

"Ow!" she screeched. "Like, what the heck!"

"What happened?" Mr. Terupt instantly *twisted* (dollar word) around.

"Like, someone just hit me right in my tushie with their square," Alexia cried.

"The ol' buttocks again, huh," Mr. Terupt said. "You okay?"

"Yes," Alexia said.

Mr. Terupt turned and looked out at us. We were laughing our heads off, and I swear I saw him smile as he shook his head at the whole scene. "Peter, come over here, please," he said.

"Why me?" Peter complained.

"Because we all know how much you like the buttocks area, don't we?"

Classic Mr. Terupt. Instead of blowing up, he was funny about it, but in a serious way. He sat Peter out for the rest of the activity and had a talk with him. Peter didn't pretend to be innocent. But like I said, I think this set us up for later. The whole thing seemed funny. No one got hurt. Peter sat out. That was it.

Once we finished tossing and counting, we headed inside, where we learned how to average all our data. Then we took our average number and used it to predict the soccer field total by figuring out how many of our squares could fit inside the field.

The number of blades of grass in our soccer field equals $77,537,412$. This isn't an exact answer, of course, but it is an accurate estimate based on all our calculations. Phew! I learned so much doing that project. It wasn't the stupid easy stuff I was used to getting from my teachers, that's for sure. We were math *wizards* (dollar word).

Jessica

Act 3, Scene 1

Things weren't going well. I had betrayed Alexia by being nice to Danielle, thinking that this was what Belle Teal would have done, and then Danielle suddenly turned on me. Without warning. I knew Alexia was behind it. I was alone—except for the friends I had in my books, like Belle—and Anna.

In November Mr. Terupt introduced us to a book that the whole class would be reading, *The Summer of the Swans* by Betsy Byars. I had never read this one—or anything by Ms. Byars, for that matter.

"This book won the Newbery Medal back in 1971," Mr. Terupt said. He held the book up. "It's not full of action like you guys tend to think of action, but it is a beautifully written book that's going to give us an awful lot to think about, learn from, and maybe even change because of."

I straightened up. I was excited. Peter moaned. As for Alexia—well, she was somewhere in la-la land. The boys made faces and the girls exchanged glances. Then Mr. Terupt went a step further.

"We're not just going to read this book," he said. "We're going to do an activity with it. An ongoing activity. More like an experience."

Now even Alexia was listening, back from outer space.

"What kind of activity?" Peter demanded. "Not some sort of stupid book project, I hope. I hate those."

"No. No project. I don't really like those things, either," Mr. Terupt said.

What did he have in mind? I wondered.

"You're going to make us dress up as a character, aren't you?" Alexia said. "Oh, I love doing that."

"Get real," Peter said.

"Will you guys be quiet and let Terupt finish," Jeffrey said.

That worked. No more interruptions, and Mr. Terupt continued.

"I want you guys to *think* about this book. In the story, there's a boy with Down syndrome—that's a mental disorder—named Charlie, and his older sister, not much older than you guys, named Sara. They have a pretty special relationship. That's what I want all of you to think about." Mr. Terupt stopped for a second, yet somehow we stayed quiet. He continued, "So what you're going to do is visit our Collaborative Classroom downstairs over the next few weeks. You'll go in groups, in the mornings and the afternoons, and simply spend time with these children doing what it is that they do."

"Mr. Terupt." I raised my hand. "What exactly is the Collaborative Classroom?" Still being relatively new to the school, I didn't know.

"It's where the retards go," Peter said.

Alexia laughed.

"I hope you'll answer that question a little differently after this experience, Peter," Mr. Terupt said, his tone very serious. Peter didn't say another word. "It's a classroom for children with a range of special needs, Jessica," Mr. Terupt continued. "Some of you are probably a little nervous or even scared. That's why you'll go in groups. I hope you'll feel different afterward, too."

Act 3, Scene 2

My group consisted of Anna and Jeffrey. I still hadn't quite figured Jeffrey out. On the other hand, I'd been eating lunch with Anna ever since being ostracized by Alexia and her clan. Danielle was back in; I was out. But I didn't want back in. I much preferred my time with Anna. She's quiet, but she's a lot smarter than everyone thinks. She's the only girl smart enough to stay out of Alexia's nonsense. Her mom's advice, she told me. We haven't talked about her mom or any of the stuff I learned from Danielle, and I haven't told her anything about me, either. For now, we've kept our secrets, and that's okay. I like Anna. She'd make a great friend to a character in a book, or in one of Dad's plays. I know she's going to be a great friend of mine.

We were very quiet on our first trip downstairs. Not one of us uttered a single sound. My hands longed to hold a book, but I hadn't brought one, so I bit at my fingernails and cuticles instead. It's funny how when you're anxious to get somewhere the journey seems to take forever, and when you're not too anxious the journey is over in no time. My journey from California lasted about as long as a ride on the Viper roller coaster, and our journey to the Collaborative Classroom took no time at all, either.

When we arrived, it was clear the teacher was expecting us.

"Hi, guys," she said. "Welcome to our Collaborative Classroom. I'm Miss Kelsey." We introduced ourselves and then she led us inside. "This is Joey." Miss Kelsey pointed to a little boy with boogers all over his face. "Can you say hi to our friends, Joey?" Miss Kelsey asked. Joey waved in our direction. A gigantic smile stretched across his face. "And this is James over here," Miss Kelsey said, pointing to a different boy. James looked pretty normal to me. He didn't say hi to us, though. He didn't even look at us. "This is Emily over here." The little girl Miss Kelsey pointed to was very cute. She had drool all over her face and hands and arms, and she moaned a lot. A different teacher used sign language as she tried to communicate with Emily. The teacher struggled to maintain eye contact with her. She told Emily to say hi. "That's Mrs. Warner helping Emily right now." Emily tried to say hi to us, but I could tell she wasn't particularly good at talking.

There were a few other children in the room and Miss Kelsey eventually introduced us to all of them. I became distracted at this point because Jeffrey had walked over to Joey and started playing the game Memory with him. I couldn't believe it. I heard him say, "That's a great job, Joey. You're really smart." And Joey smiled. Anna and I were on our way out with Miss Kelsey and James and Emily to help them do their "jobs." Before we left the room I saw Joey giving Jeffrey a big hug.

Act 3, Scene 3

Jobs turned out to be sorting the plastic forks, spoons, straws, and napkins for the cafeteria. Miss Kelsey poured the utensils on the table and James said, "Seven hundred twelve." I looked at Anna, puzzled.

"What do you mean, James?" I asked.

"Seven hundred twelve," he said again, looking down at the table.

"Does he always say seven hundred twelve?" I asked. I figured he was yelling out random numbers.

"No, James is telling us that there are seven hundred twelve utensils on the table," Miss Kelsey said.

"Seven hundred twelve utensils on the table," James repeated, this time looking at Anna and me and swaying a little as he stood.

"Great job, James!" Miss Kelsey sounded so excited. "You looked at our friends when you said that!"

"Miss Kelsey, do you mean James is right?" Anna asked. "Are there really seven hundred twelve? Is it the same amount every day or something?"

"Well, I haven't actually counted them to double-check, and no, it's not always seven hundred twelve, but James has never been wrong before," Miss Kelsey said.

Anna and I exchanged astonished looks. I was confused. James had done this amazing counting, but Miss Kelsey seemed more excited that he had looked at me. I wanted to ask questions, but decided to wait. I didn't know if asking was appropriate.

We finished up the jobs and walked back to get Jeffrey.

Act 3, Scene 4

Jeffrey was still playing with Joey, as well as a couple of other kids now. He was helping them paint.

"Jeffrey," I said. He looked up. "We have to go back now."

"Oh. Okay." His shoulders slumped. He turned to the kids. "I've got to go, guys. I'll be back soon." Then it was hug time again.

We thanked Miss Kelsey and headed back upstairs. We didn't talk on the way through the halls. I think we each had too many thoughts in our brains. By the time we reached our classroom, Jeffrey was grumpy Jeffrey again. Our very own Dr. Jekyll and Mr. Hyde, I thought.

Jeffrey

Peter called them retards, and Alexia laughed, like it was funny or somethin'. I shoulda just punched them then. It's a good thing they weren't in my group.

I went downstairs with Jessica and Anna. They seemed a little scared, but I didn't say anything.

We walked into Miss Kelsey's class and met the kids. They were great! Joey was full of love! All he wanted to do was play and hug me. He didn't get upset about anything. Not even winning or losing when we played games. James was readin' this big book when we first walked in. I could tell he was real smart. I figured he was autistic right away, 'cause he didn't look at us or say a word. And little Emily was so cute. She needed lots of help, but who wouldn't want to help her. They reminded me of Michael. Just like the Collaborative kids, Michael had the power to make you feel really good whenever you were with him. Love poured from him.

I've never told anyone about Michael, and wasn't gonna, but Jessica knew somethin' was up. She's pretty smart. She notices things.

After we visited the Collaborative Classroom a few times, she came up to me at recess one day. I was sitting at the edge of the field, out where no one else ever comes. I was lookin' through my football cards, putting them in piles by position.

"You have a secret, don't you, Jeffrey?" she said to me as she sat down.

"What are you talkin' about?" I said.

"Who do you know with special needs?"

I kept sorting my cards. I tried to ignore her. I wasn't gonna tell her anything. Then she moved closer.

"I've got a secret no one knows about, too. No one, not anyone at this school," she said.

"So why would you tell me?" I asked, lookin' at her this time.

"I was reading this book, *Ida B,* and in it the girl finally talks a little about her secret and it helps her out."

"You're always reading," I said.

"The characters help me understand and think about things," she said. "They help me know what to do."

QBs. Where was that pile? "Is that why you handle Alexia differently than any of the other girls?" I said.

"I guess so."

"Well, you can tell me your secret. I'm listenin'."

"Can I look at some of those cards while I talk?" She reached for my running backs pile.

"No!" I pushed her hand away. "Nobody ever touches my cards." She was quiet. I mighta scared her a little. "Sorry," I said.

"I'll just hold my book, then." She was quiet for a minute. I waited, and she took a big breath. "My dad didn't come to Connecticut with us," she said. "He directs plays and found a girlfriend at his work. A beautiful actress from one of his productions. My mom decided we needed to get away from California and my father . . . so here we are."

I kept sorting my cards, but I was listenin', and Jessica knew I was. After a few seconds she kept talkin'. She had more to get off her chest.

"I didn't want to come, but my mom told me I had no choice. Boy, was I ever angry with her. Angry like I've never been before. I figured my dad was dumping her, not me, so why did I have to leave, too? Silly, right? I could never live without my mom."

I stayed busy with my cards 'cause I didn't know what else to do. I didn't want to ruin it for Jessica. She had a lot to tell. So I stayed quiet.

"What I didn't know at the time was that my dad wasn't only dumping my mom, he was dumping me, too. The last time I talked to him was back in the beginning of the school year. He phoned to talk to me, but he hasn't called since."

I knew what it was like to have a parent that didn't talk to you. I had two. But I didn't know what to say, so I said nothin'. Then recess ended.

ANNA

I was pretty scared when Mr. Terupt first told us about going to the Collaborative Classroom. I didn't know those kids, only that they were gross and messy. But I didn't complain.

I was happy when I found out Jessica was in my group. She and I have been eating lunch together. She's always reading and she's smart, but she doesn't act like a know-it-all. She tells me about her books if I ask, without giving away too much of the story. I wasn't expecting or looking for a special friend, but Jessica showed up this year all the way from California, and I like her a lot. I'd like to ask her over to my house, but no one has ever come over before. I'm not sure what Mom would think. I'll have to think about it some more.

Jeffrey was in our group, too. All I know about him is that he always seems mad at everyone.

That wasn't how it turned out, though. Jeffrey was nice with the kids. Really nice. And I didn't feel scared, because Miss Kelsey and Jessica were with me. Miss Kelsey knew I was nervous, and she helped me get used to everything a little at a time. I noticed she didn't wear a wedding ring. Mr. Terupt had a lot of options.

Little Emily was so cute. I didn't want to touch her hands because she always had them in her mouth and had slobbery spit all over them, but Miss Kelsey gave us this handkerchief to wipe her up with every once in a while, and then it was okay to touch her. I held her hand on the way to do jobs and on the way back. She smiled at me, and then I felt like I was going to cry. I hadn't expected that.

One day, after everybody had been to visit the Collaborative Classroom at least once, Mr. Terupt decided we needed to discuss our group experiences.

"Mr. Terupt," I said, before we got into a serious discussion, "did you know that Miss Kelsey doesn't wear a wedding ring?"

"Is that so?"

"Yes, and neither does Ms. Newberry from across the hall."

"I did know that, but thanks for those observations, Anna."

Then Peter started in, "Oooh, Terupt and Newberry sitting in a tree, K-I-S-S-I-N-G."

"Okay, Peter. Ha-ha." Mr. Terupt held up his hands. "Enough of the matchmaking, though I appreciate your looking out for me, Anna. Now, how about sharing your experiences?"

I wanted to tell Mr. Terupt that my mom didn't have a wedding ring, but he'd moved on.

Jessica was the first to speak up. "Mr. Terupt, why is James in that room? He seems really smart."

"Yeah," Peter said, "he knew how many forks and stuff were on the table without even counting them. You should do some math with him, Luke."

"Not exactly a retard, then, huh, Peter?" Mr. Terupt said.

"No." Peter's voice lowered and so did his head.

"He's autistic," Jeffrey said.

No one said anything, probably because we were so shocked that Jeffrey had spoken at all. And because we didn't know what he meant.

"James has some things that he's really into, and he knows everything about them," Jeffrey went on. "A lot of autistic people have a special talent. James is great with numbers. But he has his problems, too."

"Hey, we should have had him tell us how many blades of grass were in the soccer field," Peter said.

"Yeah, and like, then I never woulda got hit in the tushie," Lexie told him.

Peter grinned. "But that was the best part."

"All right, all right, you two. That's enough," Mr. Terupt said.

"How do you know all that stuff, Jeffrey?" I said, even before I knew I was asking the question. I felt instantly bad. Jeffrey wasn't looking for extra attention.

Jeffrey didn't answer. He was quiet again.

Danielle

Lexie was in my group going to the Collaborative kids. Part of me was happy about that. Part of me wasn't. Things were a little confusing.

Every time we went to the Collaborative Classroom, and every time we came back, Lexie would talk bad about Jessica—even Anna sometimes.

"Don't you think Anna belongs in this room? She's, like, so stupid," Lexie said one day.

Even if I wasn't supposed to be friends with Anna, I knew she wasn't stupid. I knew because she was my plant partner, and she helped me a lot during that unit. Plus, Anna was the only girl not involved in Lexie's schemes, which made her brave, too.

"Like, Jessica should just stay down here. She doesn't have any normal friends," Lexie said.

The weirdest thing of all was that Lexie was really nice to the boys and girls in the Collaborative Classroom. Joey loved her. Okay, Joey loved everyone, but he always smiled and hugged Lexie. And she was really patient with Emily, too. Seeing Lexie like that helped me feel more comfortable in the room, and I had a good time with the kids—especially James.

Jeffrey told us that James had certain things he was really into, and one of them was farms. His brain was crammed with information about tractors and machines and cows and milking. So I brought in a bunch of pictures from home and James went nuts. He spouted off facts nonstop as he looked at each picture.

"Udders. These are the cow's udders. Clean her off and use teat dip. . . ."

Next picture.

"Hay. Find it in bales or rolls. It's hard work to hay. Throw the bale off the wagon and put it on the elevator. Stack the bales in the hayloft. . . ."

Next picture.

"John Deere tractor. Classic green and yellow. Lots of horsepower . . ."

James talked more to himself than anyone else, but that was okay. His mind was racing. When our time was up, I tried to take the pictures and he started screaming. Really screaming, not words, just noise—really loud noise. It scared me. I let go of the pictures and Mrs. Warner came right over. I got out of the way. "He can keep them," I said.

"That's very nice of you, sweetie," Mrs. Warner said. "James, can you say thank you to your friend?"

"Aargh!" James yelled, and struggled to free his body from Mrs. Warner.

"James has a hard time knowing when time is up and switching to another activity," she said.

I felt bad for James, watching him have this meltdown. "It's okay," I said, "you can keep the pictures, James. Bye."

More yelling and crying and screaming. I hoped he would calm down soon, but I had to leave. I wanted to go. I didn't like seeing that.

The whole situation upset me, and I think that was what gave me the courage to say something. We had just gone out into the hall when Lexie started right in.

"Like, what a weirdo. We better fix him up with Jessica. She's the weirdest one in our class."

"Just stop it!" I exploded. "Why do you always have to be so mean? You're nice in the room with them. Why do you have to be mean now?" Fighting back tears, I turned and ran down the hall.

"He likes cows," Lexie yelled after me. "Maybe he should date a cow like you, then."

Hot tears streamed down my cheeks. I ran upstairs and into our bathroom. Jessica was there.

"Are you okay?" she asked as I came through the door crying.

Here was my true friend. I knew it now.

"I'm sorry I've been mean to you, Jessica. I won't do it again."

She walked over to me and we hugged. I felt better.

Dear God,

It's Danielle. I know now that Jessica is my real friend. I pray that you can help Alexia not be so mean. And I pray for James. He was awful upset today. Please help him feel better and learn to handle when time is up. Thanks. Amen.

Alexia

Like, Peter knew what he was doing out there on that soccer field—hitting me with that Frisbee. So, like, I was constantly reminding him that he had killed our plant. "I told ya so," I kept telling him. Yesterday he told me to stop annoying him.

Peter's always picking on me. I bet it's because he likes me. Like, all the boys think I'm pretty. They like my fancy clothes and sparkly lip gloss. They sure don't look at Danielle. Like, she got so upset with me. She's never yelled at me before. Must be she's getting braver as she gets fatter. I'll have to fix things with her again.

I do like going to the Collaborative Classroom. I don't have to worry about things down there. The kids in that room love you no matter what. It's nice. Teach had a good idea with that one. Joey likes my feather boas. I always wear them to his class so he can see them. Like, I think I'm going to ask if I can put some lip gloss on Emily. I think maybe she'll like it. Like, every girl should try some lip gloss.

december

Peter

Last month Mr. T told us we had to read some stupid book and go spend time with the retards. That was what I thought at first, anyways. That was what I had always thought. The Collaborative Classroom was where the retards went to school. I guess it was James who made me change my mind. I mean, *The Summer of the Swans* was okay—sort of—but the Collaborative Classroom wasn't what I thought at all.

The kids were actually pretty cool, especially James. If something spilled on the floor, or if there was a bunch of objects spread out on the table, he could tell you how many there were just by looking at them. I mean it, he could tell you immediately. No counting required. No matter how many there were—312 forks, or 813 Legos. He always got it right. And James was kind of cool to hang out with. He gave me low fives—not high fives, because eye contact was tough for him—and we played games. I liked going to see him.

So I liked Mr. T's next idea. He never ran out of ideas.

"Okay, guys. Here's the deal," he told us in December. "We're going to have a holiday party like every other class, but it's going to be different."

"Of course," I blurted out. "That's no surprise." I do that sometimes, open my mouth before thinking. A lot of times, actually. Everybody—even Mr. T—cracked a smile, because I was right.

"You'll form small groups and work to create a center focused on a certain holiday. It might be Christmas, Ramadan, Kwanzaa, or Hanukkah." Mr. T kept going with the directions, but I didn't catch most of it. I was thinking. Then I did that blurt-out thing again.

"Mr. T, can we invite James and his friends to our party?"

Everyone was quiet and looked at me. Then Jessica said, "That's a great idea." And the rest of the class agreed. Mr. T had a smile stretched across his face. He just nodded. And I thought I saw him wipe at his eyes. I don't know why he did that, though.

Jessica

Act 4, Scene 1

I chose Ramadan as my holiday. I wanted to research something I knew very little about. I ended up in a group with Anna, Danielle, Jeffrey, and Alexia. Alexia wanted to be with Katie, Wendy, Natalie, and Heather, but Mr. Terupt didn't go for that. If he was looking for trouble, he got it.

Our task was clear. When Mr. Terupt announced the project, he said, "Your centers will need to include a research component, a game, an arts and crafts activity, and food. Your center will need to operate all by itself, because you'll be visiting the other centers when people come to visit yours."

My group started talking about who could do what, but Alexia didn't let that go on too long. "Like, you need to do the research, Jessica. 'Cause like, you're the smartest. Anna's too stupid to read that stuff."

Anna stared at the floor. She used to do a lot of that, but not as much these days. It wasn't just her head that went down this time—her entire body sagged after Alexia's nasty comment. Alexia looked at Jeffrey next, but she didn't have the nerve to say anything. Then she smiled at me and Danielle. She got nothing in return from me, but I could see Danielle half smiling.

Jeffrey and I collaborated on the research, while Anna and Danielle were in charge of designing the arts and crafts activity. I wanted to work with Jeffrey. I had shared my secret with him, and he needed another chance to share his with me. Anna and Danielle had done fine together with the plants, so I knew they'd work well together this time. Plus, I hoped Danielle would become friends with Anna despite her grandmother's warnings. Alexia named herself as our group manager. According to her, she was responsible for overseeing all of our work. Or as she put it, "Like, I'll just watch and make sure everybody is doing what they're supposed to do. I'll be, like, our manager." I think she meant *boss*.

We went along with Alexia's grand plan because it was easier not to have her involved in our tasks. But that wasn't good enough for Alexia. No, she tried her best to get everyone mad at each other. That's what she was all about.

Act 4, Scene 2

One day during project time I was meeting with Jeffrey and Anna, discussing how to put our center together. Danielle was nearby organizing the arts and crafts materials that she and Anna had been working tirelessly to create. Then Alexia made her move.

"Like, don't you guys think Danielle should be in charge of the food?" Alexia said loud enough for Danielle to hear. I braced myself for what was coming next. "I mean, just look at her. Like, she's so fat, she must be good with food."

Danielle hurried out of the room. None of us said or did anything. It was as if we thought pretending nothing had happened would make everything better. It didn't. My turn to be hurt came next. Alexia didn't spare me.

Act 4, Scene 3

Jeffrey and I decided that making a trivia game about Ramadan was the perfect way for people to learn about our holiday and what we'd researched. It took loads of work. We had just finished writing all our research as questions on the trivia cards.

Enter Alexia. She must have just come from the bathroom. She wore fresh shiny lip gloss and chewed on a new piece of gum. She paraded over to us with an exaggerated hip motion in her jean skirt and zebra tights, bent down, and grabbed some of the trivia cards. She looked them over, but I don't think she read any of them. She snapped her gum that she wasn't supposed to have.

"Like, nobody's gonna understand these questions." She stared right at me. "Nobody ever understands you, not with all your stuck-up words. Like, you just want to make everyone else feel stupid. You think you're so smart." She flicked the card at me.

That wasn't true. I didn't try to do that.

Act 4, Scene 4

Enter Mr. Terupt.

"Alexia."

I looked up. I didn't even know he was there. Alexia didn't, either. She spun around, alarmed.

"I think it's time for you to follow me."

He escorted her out of the room. They were gone for a while.

Act 4, Scene 5

Enter Mr. Terupt, without Alexia. Where was she?

"I need to talk to the four of you now," he said, looking at Jeffrey, Danielle, Anna, and me. We sat down in our project area.

"I've watched Alexia be unpleasant to all of you. I hoped that one of you was going to stand up to her and tell her to stop. You didn't."

I looked down. I knew I should have done something. I wasn't strong like the friends in my books.

"If you let people get away with being mean, they're going to keep being mean. You need to stick up for each other. Even Alexia isn't tough enough to make fun of you—not if all four of you stick together."

I could feel Mr. Terupt's eyes on me. He leaned forward, trying to peer up into my face. He tried to make eye contact with each of us. We all stared at the floor.

"You should be disappointed," he said. "You should stand by each other. That's what being friends is all about."

Still, we sat quiet. Anna wiped her eyes. So did Danielle.

"Don't sit and pout," Mr. Terupt said. "That won't help

anything. You need to keep working. Learn from this and don't make the same mistake again."

Exit Mr. Terupt.

Act 4, Scene 6

What was Jeffrey thinking? I wondered. What were Danielle and Anna feeling?

"I'm never talking to Alexia again," Danielle said.

"Me, neither," Anna added.

"That's no better," I said. "We don't have to be friends with her, but we can't shut her out. We have to be bigger people." I looked down again. I felt as disappointed in myself as Mr. Terupt did in all of us. I wasn't brave enough.

LUKE

Our bathroom is positioned directly across the hall from our classroom. Who cares, right? I'd never thought anything of it until the day I felt trapped out there. I saw the *shakedown* (dollar word), all compliments of Peter.

I was in the classroom working on my holiday center. All my materials were spread out on the floor, and I was busy calculating the proper dimensions for my gameboard. Mr. Terupt was on the other side of the room checking in with a different group. I didn't notice Peter. I stretched out on my belly and worked the math. The soles of my sneaks pointed up—a great invitation for mess-around Peter. I never felt a thing. He's definitely sneaky. I sometimes wonder what's the *likelihood* (dollar word) Peter will grow up to be a world-famous thief. I had no clue anything was even happening until I heard the giggling and Peter said, "Hey, Luke, what kind of sneaks are those? Elmer's?"

I popped my head up. "What are you talking about?"

"Better be careful. If you try to go anywhere in those, you might get stuck."

I looked back at my feet. Mess-around Peter had struck. The bottoms of my sneakers were completely covered in Elmer's glue.

"You jerk," I said, without any real authority. Truth is, I didn't really care. It wasn't worth getting upset over. Besides, I'm sort of used to Peter's antics. I thought they were always harmless. I untied my shoes and placed them next to me— bottoms up, of course—until I finished my math. Peter's victory celebration was cut short by my easy solution. Maybe I don't get upset with Peter because I know I'll always outwit him. This drives him nuts, and I love it.

Once I finished my calculations, I grabbed my sneakers and headed to the bathroom. Mr. Terupt was still busy with a different group so he didn't see any of Peter's shenanigans or me leaving the classroom. I held my shoes under the sink and washed off the glue. Then I wiped the soles dry with a paper towel and put my sneakers back on. I pushed the bath- room door open and quickly jumped back inside. I was trapped.

Mr. Terupt was having a conference with someone out in the hall. I pushed the door open just a crack to see who it was.

"You've done it your way," he said. Mr. Terupt had his back to me. He was leaning forward, talking to the person against the wall. "Now you'll do it my way." He straightened up and folded his arms. He meant business. And that was when I saw who it was.

Black and purple streaks covered her cheeks, a combination of her makeup and tears. Alexia—crying. I had never seen or heard of Alexia crying before.

"I like you, Lexie. I want some of your classmates to like you, too. I'm trying to help. I want you to be *friendlier* [dollar word]. I will *not* tolerate your meanness anymore."

Wow! Was this really going to work?

"Go into the bathroom and wash your face. Come back when you're ready. Is there anything you want to say before I go back in?"

Alexia stormed past Mr. Terupt without looking at him, and without saying a word. Mr. Terupt let out a big sigh and shook his head. Then he walked back into the classroom. I wonder what he was thinking. I decided not to say anything about my sneakers. It didn't seem important. Mr. Terupt had more serious matters on his plate, like *discipline* (dollar word).

I waited a few minutes before following Mr. Terupt into the classroom. I didn't want it to seem obvious that I'd been eavesdropping, but I was eager to tell somebody about what I had just seen. That's why I think I walked into the classroom a little rushed and wasn't really paying attention. Even if I had been, it probably would have happened.

I'd barely walked through the door before I stepped in a puddle of water. My feet went up and my arms flew out. I flailed like an ostrich trying to catch its balance. Somehow I managed to stay upright after sliding across the linoleum floor to the carpet. Mr. Terupt was having a serious conversation with Jessica, Danielle, Jeffrey, and Anna, so he didn't see any of this. But Peter, Ben, Nick, and some of the other guys rolled around in hysterics. I knew what they had done. Or should I say what *Peter* had done. He likes to put his thumb over the opening of the drinking *fountain* (dollar word) and push the button. It's another one of his infamous stunts. This one makes the water shoot all the way to the door. That was how the puddle miraculously appeared on the floor. Whether Peter meant to have the water on the floor, or if it just ended up there after he sprayed someone else, I don't know. Either way, it doesn't matter. I didn't have time to do anything about it, because someone else came through the door just after me.

She must have been making her rounds, going from class to class, just to visit for a few minutes. Today was her unlucky day. Mrs. Williams took one step into our classroom and hit the water. I felt sorry for her. She was wearing a navy blue suit (a jacket and skirt) with high heels. She wasn't able to keep her balance. Her foot shot way out to the side as soon as it touched the puddle. I thought she was going to do a split, but then her other foot touched the water and slid forward. Mrs. Williams fell backward with her arms grabbing empty air. She landed smack on her back, right in the water, with her legs stuck in the air. That was when I saw my principal's underwear.

I couldn't believe it. I knew I shouldn't keep staring but I couldn't look away. We all gawked at her multicolored flower underwear. And that's not the best of it—or the worst of it, if you're Mrs. Williams. Her underwear was a bit discombobulated. In other words, she had a wedgie! It was unbelievable! I'll never forget it, not as long as I live. I swear it. It was the day I saw my principal's underwear, and more.

Mr. Terupt rushed over to help her. The rest of us fought to keep from laughing. It was our principal, after all. Even Peter wasn't snickering. He actually looked nervous.

"Mrs. Williams, are you okay?" Mr. Terupt said, helping her to her feet. "Peter, get some towels to wipe this water up."

Why did he pick Peter? Because he knew Peter's antics led to the water being on the floor. I'm sure it was his way of letting Peter know he knew.

"I'm okay," Mrs. Williams said, brushing herself off and smoothing out her clothes. "Sorry for the interruption." She turned and left. How embarrassing! As soon as the door closed behind her, the laughter and whispers started.

"Clearly this can't happen again," Mr. Terupt said. "We're lucky Mrs. Williams didn't get hurt, or that someone else didn't, either. I expect we won't have water pooled on the floor like that again." Mr. Terupt looked directly at Peter after saying this. Yep, he knew. He shook his head, then walked over to his desk.

I thought for sure this event would be *unequaled* (dollar word) by any other for the rest of the year. Little did I know that something much bigger was coming our way.

Alexia

Teach was like, "Alexia, I think it's time for you to follow me."

I went into the hall with him. He closed the door behind
us. Teachers had done this stuff with me before. It was like,
no big deal.

I didn't even give Teach a chance. "They're being so
mean to me," I blurted out. "They won't let me do anything.
Jessica thinks, like, she's the boss."

But this is where Teach was different again.

"Wrong," he said. "Stop."

"But—"

He put both hands up. "Just stop," he said.

I was quiet. He looked right at me.

"You're lying. And I don't like liars," he said. "You're being mean. And I don't like mean people."

I felt real tears coming. I didn't want to cry. Not for real. I squeezed my teeth together and scrunched my eyes. I held my purse hard with both hands.

"You're acting like the meanest girl I've ever seen," he said.

I couldn't help it. The tears came. I was really upset. I looked down at the floor.

"I'm not being unreasonable, Lexie."

I was like, Yes, you are. But I didn't say anything.

"I'm telling you the truth, and sometimes the truth can hurt."

I kept my head down. I pulled a tissue from my purse and wiped my eyes. He was being a bully.

"I know you're not mean deep down inside," Teach went on. "So stop acting like you are. Miss Kelsey has told me some amazing things about you in her room."

He didn't get it. Nobody was gonna be my friend. I know, because that's how it was before. Kids made fun of me, because of my clothes, because of how I talked. Leopard Lexie and Lexie Like, they called me. And then one day in third grade I attacked back. I yelled at some girl like Mom and Dad yelled at each other. And after that, no one wanted to be friends with her. It didn't matter that what I said was a lie. They ditched her and became my friends instead. Just like that, I became the leader. All of a sudden I was getting all kinds of attention, unlike at home. Mom was around, but usually too upset over Dad ('cause he was never around) to worry about me. And then last year, she, like, hit her limit, and threw Dad out of the house. Mom told me then, "Alexia, don't let people push you around like your father did to us. You take charge and fight back." So there's no way I'm going back to being nice. Nobody's gonna make fun of me again.

I don't remember anything else Mr. Terupt said. I was too mad to listen.

I *hate* you, Mr. Terupt.

Jeffrey

"Did it help?" I asked Jessica one day in our Ramadan group. We were just doing some research on the computer.

"What?" she asked.

"Did tellin' help, like Ida B?"

"I think it helped a little," she said.

I stared at the computer.

"I'm listening," she said

"You won't tell anyone?" I said.

"I won't tell," she said. "Promise."

"'Cause nobody knows any of this. I just moved here last year, halfway through the school year, and nobody knows anything about me."

"I won't tell," she said again.

I'm not sure why I believed her, but for the first time ever, I told someone my secret.

"My brother's name was Michael. The football cards were his. He was older than me. He had Down syndrome and leukemia, and was real sick, so my parents had me in order to save him."

I could feel Jessica looking at me after telling her that last part, but I kept starin' at the computer.

"They gave Michael my stem cells—special cells that can turn into anything else in your body—hoping that they would become what Michael needed. It worked for a while, but then he got sick again. He was in and out of the hospital a lot, so that's how I learned about kids with special needs."

I stopped. The computer was quiet. Jessica hadn't pushed anything on the keyboard. She was listenin'.

"Then the summer before fourth grade I gave my bone marrow to Michael. It was his last chance. Everything else had failed."

I stopped again. My throat was tightening around the lump in it. It was gonna be hard to tell the rest.

"What happened?" Jessica said.

"It worked, but not fast enough. Michael got sick before his body could fight the cancer off. . . . I didn't save him."

The screen saver bounced around. I stared at it. Then Jessica said somethin' no one had ever said to me before.

"It's not your fault, Jeffrey."

I got up and walked to the bathroom. I had to.

anna

I never had a teacher stick up for me before. I'd get picked on and made fun of, and my teachers never did anything. Maybe because I never did anything, either. I didn't cry or get upset, I just stayed quiet. Maybe it seemed like it didn't bother me, but nobody's got skin that thick.

Mr. Terupt did something. I loved him for that. He wasn't real happy about it, though. He wanted us to do the sticking up for each other. I didn't know if I could do that. But with Jessica and Danielle by my side, I knew I'd try. Mr. Terupt was right about that.

Things were much easier in our group after the whole Alexia incident. She came back quiet and remained quiet for the rest of the day, and every day after that. I knew she was feeling bad. A lot of girls had felt the same way because of her, so I figured it was only fair. But it bothered me, too. Mom has always told me, "We don't have enough days to waste being upset or sad. You've got to be happy and have fun, Anna." I think Mom's positive attitude is pretty amazing—especially after all she's been through—and I think she's right. We weren't mean to Alexia, but we left her alone. I hoped she'd be different now that Mr. Terupt had held a conference with her.

During the time we worked on our center, I found the courage to do something I hadn't ever done before. One day during recess—while doing some stick sketching in the dirt—I took a deep breath and plunged ahead.

"Would you guys like to come over to my house for a playdate?" I asked Jessica and Danielle.

Jessica looked up. "I'd love to," she said. She glanced at Danielle, who kept her head down and continued sketching. Danielle's really good at drawing, so I thought maybe she just wanted to finish her sketch. *Snap!* Her stick broke in half. "But I'll need to check with my mom first," Jessica added.

"Me too," Danielle said, but she still didn't look up. "Let me ask my mom."

"You don't have to come over if you don't want to," I said to Danielle.

"No! I want to," she said, looking right at me this time. I believed her. Then she looked away. "But I need to get permission."

The recess whistle blew. Danielle had drawn three girls holding hands in the dirt. I smiled. They both wanted to come over. I just hoped their mothers said yes.

Danielle

The holiday centers turned out great. It was a lot of hard work, especially with Alexia in our group, but Mr. Terupt took care of her. She wasn't the same after that. She became real quiet—which helped us get our center put together smoothly.

Jessica and Jeffrey completed the trivia game. They came up with some really great questions. Luke loved playing it when he visited our holiday. He said he learned a lot from it, which Mr. Terupt was happy to hear.

Mr. Terupt hung around our center because of the cookies. I made them, even after what Alexia said about me. My mom and grandma helped me find a recipe that used cumin, which is a spice. The three of us spend a lot of time together in the kitchen. It was the perfect opportunity to ask about going to Anna's. But . . . I just couldn't get myself to do it.

The best part of our holiday centers day took place when our Collaborative friends visited. That was Peter's great idea. Some of the games were hard for them, but we all helped. They were able to do the crafts and eat special foods, like my cookies. James liked our craft project where you had to cut thin strips of paper and staple rings together to make a long chain. The chain is a calendar to help you count down the days of Ramadan, which can be twenty-nine or thirty days long. Our chain included way more links than that because our guests kept adding them. "One hundred thirty-seven," James said after eyeing the chain for just a few seconds. Then he started attaching more links.

James really liked the surprise I had for him. I put together a collection of photographs of Middle Eastern farms and farming. He sat down and started talking about them and studying them. Seeing James like this made me happy.

Jeffrey surprised us. Once Joey showed up, Jeffrey pulled out this little memory game that he had made, with pairs of matching cards with different Ramadan pictures on them. He and Joey played.

It was a super wonderful day. Mr. Terupt was smiling. So was I.

Jessica

Act 5, Scene 1

"Hi, honey. How was school?" Mom asked as I climbed into the car. Mom was great about giving me rides home whenever she could. Some kids, like Jeffrey, had to ride the bus every day.

Mom's trying to get serious about her writing. She's already very skilled at it, having helped on some of Dad's plays back in California, but now she's writing for herself. That's why she's free in the afternoons to pick me up sometimes. We're lucky to have enough money so that my mom doesn't have to get a steady job right now—she can actually pursue her passion. I hope I can do that someday, too. Mom did get a part-time job at a local bookstore, so she can interact with people and keep her mind from wandering back to California. My mind still wanders back there, but not like it did a few months ago. My dad hasn't called again.

"School was fine," I said. I buckled my seat belt and away we drove. "Mom, you've heard me talk about Anna and Danielle, right?"

"Yes. Is something wrong?" Mom stepped on the brakes harder than usual and we jerked to a halt at the stop sign.

I shook my head. "Nothing's wrong," I said. I looked my way. "Coast is clear." Mom eased off the brakes. "Anna asked Danielle and me over to her house."

"That's great, Jessica," Mom said.

"Yes, but I know Danielle won't be going."

"How do you know that?"

I filled Mom in on what I knew about Anna's mother. And I explained why Danielle's mom wouldn't allow Danielle to associate with the likes of Anna. Mom turned right onto our road.

"Well, I'm not going to say no just because Anna's mother made a mistake once." We pulled into our driveway and Mom put the car in park. "If Danielle is a nice girl, I bet her mother is, too," Mom said. "But we'll make up our own minds about what kind of person Anna's mother really is."

"Dad made a mistake. You didn't want to give him another chance," I said.

"Your father didn't want another chance," Mom said. "He made that clear before we left." She paused. "The divorce papers came today."

I sat all quiet. Mom's bluntness really zapped me.

"I'm sorry, honey," Mom said. "I'm sure your father will call soon."

I shrugged. "You don't need to lie to make me feel better."

"Okay, you're right." She sighed. "I've always been honest and up-front with you." Another sigh. "I don't know if he'll call."

january

Jessica

Act 6, Scene 1

Anna's house was small but cozy, just the right size for her and her mother. It was painted white with gray shutters, and there was a nice front porch. Anna met us there. We said our hellos and before I knew it, my mom was shaking hands with Terri (that's Anna's mom). Terri invited my mom in for a cup of coffee and they disappeared into the kitchen. Anna led me to her bedroom.

"I hope our moms become friends," I said.

"Me too," Anna said. "My mom doesn't have any."

Neither does mine, I thought. In California, my dad was always the one working and socializing, while my mom hung out with me. We didn't see him much. Even back then, he was very busy. He called the other day and asked Mom if she'd received the divorce papers. That was it. He didn't even ask to talk to me.

"You're reading *Belle Teal*," I said to Anna. I saw the book sitting on her nightstand. "Do you like it?"

"I do," Anna said. "Mom brought it home for me from the library where she works."

I didn't know Terri worked in a library. How exciting. I wanted to talk to her about books. And then Anna told me that her mother was taking some art classes. She showed me some of her mom's artwork. Amazing! I immediately thought of Danielle, and hoped she would get a chance to meet Terri and discover for herself the connection they shared. After that Anna showed me the rest of her books and her rock collection. Then I taught her how to make worry dolls, something I'd learned about from one of the characters in a book I read. I figured the dolls could worry about my dad, because I was done with that. Our playdate was perfect and it flew by like a day at the amusement park. We said our thank-yous and good-byes and agreed to do it again.

Driving home, Mom said, "What you heard about Terri was right. Poor girl."

I stayed quiet. After seeing Terri myself, I knew the story was right. She looked very young.

"I told her about your father," Mom said.

I remained quiet. I didn't know how to feel. Surprised. Angry. Happy. I felt all of these at the same time. Mom was quiet now, too. I guess we were busy thinking to ourselves.

ΑΝΝΑ

Danielle wasn't able to come to my first playdate because of bad timing, but Jessica made it. We had a blast! Jessica's mom drove her over, but instead of dropping Jessica off and leaving, she came to our front door and accepted Mom's invitation for a cup of coffee.

I was really glad. My mom never has anyone over, so it turned out to be her first playdate, too. Maybe she was done paying for her "mistake" now. I sure hoped so. And since I was the "mistake," I felt like it was my fault. I wanted to help her find a friend, and a husband.

The afternoon flew by.

After Jessica and her mother left, Mom pulled me into a hug. "Those are genuine people, Anna," she said. "You've found a good friend there. You can get as close to her as you want."

Mom's words made me smile. I hoped Danielle could come the next time. I was sure Mom would think the same of her.

Danielle

"Class meeting," Mr. Terupt announced.

This was one of my favorite times in the classroom. We all moved our desks out of the way and made a circle with our chairs. Everybody sat in the circle, even Mr. Terupt. He held on to the microphone. It wasn't a real microphone, but we used it as our talking object. You can only speak when you have the microphone. I waited for Mr. Terupt to get us started.

"It looks like our chain should touch the floor soon, as long as you guys can give me another great day or two," Mr. Terupt said.

The chain was our class reward system. Mr. Terupt had hung a single link from the ceiling on the first day of school, and he attached a link each time we had an outstanding day as a class. Our goal was to get the chain to touch the floor, at which point we'd earn a free day.

"You've done super so far," Mr. Terupt said. "So I'm wondering what you'd like to do for your free day."

Mr. Terupt passed the mike to his left. You didn't have to say anything if you didn't want to. Alexia passed it along to the next person. Ever since Mr. Terupt had taken her out into the hall, she hadn't said anything.

Luke was the first one to make a great suggestion. "Why can't we just have time to do whatever we want? It'd be like indoor recess, but we could plan it better, and just have free time."

"I like Luke's idea," Jeffrey piped up when he got the mike. "If it's free time, maybe James and Joey and Emily, or any of the Collaborative kids, could come up for a little bit—or, if we wanted, some of us could go down there."

"We could bring in games," Anna added, taking the mike.

Then it was my turn. "I think we should do what everyone's suggested for part of the day," I said, "but maybe we could go outside, too." Everyone cheered. It was weird, having the other girls agree with me. If Alexia had been her old self, she would have controlled them, but now that Alexia was sidelined, all the girls got along better.

Not having girl wars didn't mean everything was perfect. I still had a problem—Anna. I hadn't gone to her playdate because I'd been too chicken to ask my mom. I made up some excuse about it being a bad weekend for my family. Jessica told me she had a great time and that Anna's mom was friendly. Now Anna asked us about coming over again.

"Find out when it'll be a good weekend for your family, and we'll plan the playdate for then," Anna told me.

I've got to mention it to my mom this time. I just have to.

Mr. Terupt was last to speak at the meeting. "I like what I've heard," he said. "We could plan for part of the day to be spent inside, playing games, then we'd get some fresh air. I'll think about it some more and let you know. But first you need to earn the last link. Meeting adjourned," he said. He always ends by saying that.

I really like these meetings. The first time we had one, Mr. Terupt told us that it was a way for everyone to have a voice. I didn't get it at first, but now I do.

Peter

We finally earned a class reward. Or almost. I really hoped Mr. T would come through for us about going outside. So I shot my hand up as soon as class started the next day.

"What is it now, Peter?" Mr. T said.

"Have you thought about us going outside? The school rule says we can't go out in the snow. We can go out on the blacktop, but it's too crowded and there's nothing to do." Everyone was quiet. They listened because they knew I was right.

"Well, Peter, I like how you're thinking ahead. I did talk to Mrs. Williams, and she gave us special permission to go out in the snow as long as *everyone* has snow pants and hats and gloves and boots."

"She gave us special permission even after we all saw her underwear?" I said.

"Yes," Mr. T said, trying to move us past the giggles that started.

"Permission for the snow?" I asked again, just to make sure I had it right.

"In the snow," Mr. T said. "The key being *everyone* needs to bring their stuff, or else we can't go out."

I couldn't believe it. When I went to bed that night, I had visions of snowballs dancing in my head.

It was going to be the best class party day ever.

Jessica

Act 7, Scene 1

The class bubbled with energy. Mr. Terupt had just attached the last link needed for our paper chain to touch the floor. The links were hard to come by with the likes of Peter and Alexia in our classroom, but we did it.

"Congratulations. You've earned your free day," Mr. Terupt said. "A class party day."

Peter couldn't believe it. None of us could, really, but Peter was beside himself. The only thing he could wrap his brain around was going outside to play in the snow.

"Don't forget your snow stuff, California girl," he said to me. I didn't need reminding. It was all I could think about, but not because I was excited.

Act 7, Scene 2

I raised my hand tentatively and waited for Mr. Terupt to call on me. It was nearly time to go home. I couldn't wait any longer.

"You have a question, Jessica?"

"Yes . . . sort of," I said. "I have a problem. I don't have any snow pants. I didn't need them in California."

Silence. It was like I sucked all the excitement out of the classroom with a gigantic vacuum hose. Peter glared at me. I couldn't look at him. Then I saw Luke raise his hand. Mr. Terupt called on him.

"Lukester."

"I have a pair of snow pants Jessica can borrow. They're my sister's old ones."

"Thatta baby, Lukester!" Peter yipped. "Saved!"

"Thanks, Lukester. That's very nice of you," Mr. Terupt said, looking in my direction. "I'm sure Jessica will take them."

I could only nod.

"Yes!" Peter yelled. "This is going to be great!"

I thought so, too—especially after Luke's generosity. I always thought Luke only cared about himself. Maybe I was wrong to prejudge him.

Mr. Terupt sat at his desk smiling. He reminded me of the old professor in *The Lion, the Witch and the Wardrobe*. Did he know everything?

LUKE

Twenty-seven links. That's how many it took for the chain to hit the floor. I was wrong. I had estimated twenty-six. Mr. Terupt had us estimate the final number when we only had five. Most everybody jotted down random guesses, but I took a ruler and measured the length of what we had and the length left to reach the floor. The real problem was that the links were all different sizes. A variable that I couldn't control. I averaged the links that were hanging and used that to help me come up with twenty-six.

"All right, gang," Mr. Terupt said. "Twenty-seven links. Let's see if anyone guessed that."

He had all our guesses stuffed in an empty coffee can. I was hoping to be the closest. Maybe nobody got it right. He pulled our little scraps of paper out one by one.

"Twenty-one. *Thirty* [dollar word]. Fifty!" Everyone laughed except me. "Twenty-three. Aha," he said. "Here's one. Twenty-seven."

I lost. I can't believe I was wrong.

"And the winner is . . . Anna."

She must have guessed. There's no way she could have figured it out. Anna walked up to Mr. Terupt with her head held high. At least the winner wasn't Peter or Alexia.

"Congratulations, Anna," Mr. Terupt said. He handed her a homework pass. She was all smiles. I didn't need one of those, anyway.

"Yay, Anna," Jessica said. "Way to go!"

"But wait," Mr. Terupt said. "There seems to be one more estimate that's correct."

"Must be Luke's," I heard someone whisper.

"Drumroll, please," Mr. Terupt said.

Baatttttttttttt!

"And the second winner is . . . Peter."

No way, I screamed inside my head. Of course Peter made a major production of walking to the front of the room and taking a dramatic bow. "Thank you. Thank you," he said. "This is a great honor."

Mr. Terupt handed him a homework pass. "Get out of here," he said. Everyone laughed, except me.

Peter flashed his homework pass in my face. The Elmer's sneakers didn't bother me, but this did. I felt hot. My face and ears burned. I turned lobster red. I could feel it. I'm going to get even, I thought.

"The chain has touched the floor," Mr. Terupt announced. "It's time for a free day." My *colleagues* (dollar word) and I were in for a treat. Mr. Terupt told us that we would be going outside. Great, I thought. But what's the catch? Was he going to tell us to bring our *shovels* (dollar word) to find out how many scoops it would take to clear the parking lot? Nope. Just snow pants, hats, boots, and *mittens* (dollar word). We had the okay from Mrs. Williams to play in the snow as long as everyone had the proper snow clothes.

Jessica threw us the curveball. And boy, was it a bender. She didn't have snow pants. Talk about hitting us with the unexpected.

So who comes to the rescue? Me. I had to. Plus, I liked Jessica. She was serious about school—and I didn't want to miss the chance to *inoculate* (dollar word) Peter with a snowball.

Jeffrey

"It's not your fault." That was what Jessica had said to me, and that was what I kept repeating in my head. The only other person to ever tell me that was Michael. It was just before he died. I have a hard time believin' it, but his words still make me feel a little better.

I need his words, and Jessica's, 'cause I know Mom and Dad blame me. They sure don't love me. Why else are they so silent? They don't speak to me—rarely, and they never speak to each other. Dad has started going to work again, but Mom mopes around the house. She hasn't been out of her pajamas since Michael's funeral.

Christmas was tough again this year. It was our second one without Michael, not that we celebrated either time. Dad got a tree this year, though. It showed up one day in our living room. I put a few decorations on it. Mom pretended it wasn't there.

february

Peter

I ran into the classroom. "Does everyone have their stuff?" I yelled.

Mr. T looked up from his desk. "Calm down, Peter," he said.

"Does everyone have their stuff?" I said again, still excited.

"Calm down," Mr. T said again. "Take a deep breath."

I took a deep breath. Then, in a normal voice I said, "Does everyone have their stuff?"

"I think so," Mr. T said.

"Let's go then. Let's go!" I said.

"We'll go out later, Peter. Besides, we need to take attendance and lunch count and listen to morning announcements." Mr. T also figured if we went out and got soaking wet first thing, we'd be miserable for the rest of the day. He had a good point, but I still wanted to get outside.

We spent the morning spread out all over the place playing different games. I played Scattergories with Mr. T, Luke, and Jeffrey. The letter *B* came up on the dice. We raced through putting down our ideas and then it was time to share. We took turns, going down the list, and then the item "Things at a beach" came up. Jeffrey shared, then Luke, then Mr. T, and then it was my turn. I leaned in and said, "Babes."

"Who brings babies to the beach?" Luke said.

"Not babies. Babes," Jeffrey said.

I almost died. But wait. It gets better. Our very own brainiac, Luke, just sat there watching us laugh. Then he said, "What do you mean?" Can you believe that? He didn't know babes. I freaked.

"Holy smokes," I said. "What rock are you living under?"

Mr. T jumped in at that point.

"Easy, Peter," Mr. T said. "Lots of girls don't appreciate that term. It sounds as if you don't respect them, and part of being a man is knowing how to respect women."

"Ohhh!" Luke said. "Girls." His lightbulb had suddenly turned on.

Mr. T looked at me and smiled, shaking his head.

Mr. T's the best, I thought. That was the last time I got to hang out with him.

LUKE

Peter thought he was so smart all of a sudden. He won a homework pass off a lucky guess and he confused me in Scattergories. Big deal. I *resolved* (dollar word) to get him.

Jeffrey

Never thought I'd play a game with my teacher, but I did. I played Scattergories with Terupt and Luke and Peter. And I learned that I'm even smarter than Luke at some things. But that doesn't make him out to be a bad kid, just a dork. As smart as he is, Luke doesn't make a stink about it. I like him for that.

But Peter. Sometimes he gets on my nerves. He's always doing stuff and never gets in trouble. I knew he was just waitin' to get outside. I had a surprise for him.

It woulda been better if I never got involved. If I just stayed hating school, none of this woulda happened.

Peter

Finally we were outside. The snow was perfect. The kind that packed and formed super snowballs. I scooped up a handful as we walked toward the field, squeezing it over and over. "No snowballs," Mr. T had told us before coming out. We reached the corner and I stuffed the snowball in my pocket. It was too perfect to just toss down. It wasn't like I was going to throw it. I ran out onto the untouched field. The field was perfect, too. There was a mountain of snow right in the middle that we climbed up.

I was already standing at the top when I saw Lexie making her way up the side. I thought about how she'd been really quiet lately, like she was down in the dumps. Maybe that was why I thought knocking her into the snow would snap her out of her trance. Without thinking it through (something I never do, anyway), I slid down the side and gave her a little shove. She tumbled backward. I laughed hard. She didn't. I ran toward a smaller mound of snow.

That was how the game started.

Everyone joined in, running back and forth between the two mounds. We knocked each other down as we ran and we wrestled each other off the tops.

I'm not sure how it happened, but somehow *I* got knocked down. I was watching out for Lexie when somebody shoulder-checked me from behind. I fell off the mountain and landed on my belly. Lexie came running over and kicked snow in my face. I was fuming. It's one thing to knock each other down, but kicking snow in someone's face . . . that's just wrong. I was angry. I got on my knees and BAM! I got knocked down on my face again. Now I was fuming and steaming. I pushed myself up to see who did it when BAM! Same thing happened. This time the person held my face down, too. I was so mad I jumped up, pulled that snowball out of my pocket, and chucked it for all I was worth.

Jessica

Act 8, Scene 1

You could hear our big, heavy snow boots thumping down the sidewalk until we turned the corner and dashed out onto the field. A monstrous hill of snow loomed right in the middle. Naturally, we all sprinted toward it and clamored to the top. Then we jumped, taking the plunge into waist-deep powdery white. It didn't take long before the boys started taking each other down.

Peter seized the opportunity and sent Alexia flying down the side of the mountain. She landed on her back, all splayed out. Peter laughed and ran. Alexia sat up and I could tell how mad she was by the lines in her contorted face. Suddenly I thought of a way to get Peter. He wouldn't expect me. He'd be keeping his eyes on Alexia, expecting her to retaliate.

I collared Danielle and Anna. "Here's what we're going to do," I said. It wasn't a suggestion, more like I simply told them how my ingenious plan would be executed.

Act 8, Scene 2

We hid behind the mountain of snow. Peter came running toward us and scampered right up the side. While Peter stood on top like the king of all dorks, we snuck up the back side of the hill.

Danielle threw her shoulder into Peter, knocking him off balance. He wavered. I blasted him with my shoulder, coming from the opposite direction. Anna gave the last little nudge from behind.

The one-two-three punch was too much for Peter to handle. He squawked like a dying seagull as he flailed through the air, landing facedown.

Alexia ran over and kicked snow in his face the instant he picked his head up. Danielle, Anna, and I had just reached the other mound when we turned around and saw Peter fire the snowball.

LUKE

Alexia kicked snow in Peter's face. He griped and whined as he sat up to wipe the snow from his eyes.

"Let's get him, Lukester," Jeffrey said. I felt like a couple of *snipers* (dollar word) sizing up our target. Jeffrey slid down the smaller mound, hurried across the snow, and shoved Peter's face back into the white powder. Peter never saw it coming, and Jeffrey was long gone by the time Peter sat up to wipe his face again. That was when I attacked. I blasted him from behind, knocking him down, and held his face in the snow extra-long. This *reversal* (dollar word) of typical roles, with me being the victor, felt awesome. It was one of the greatest *upsets* (dollar word) of all time.

My victory celebration lasted only a second before everything was *shattered* (dollar word).

Jeffrey

Peter had it comin'. I got him good and so did Lukester. They say all's fair in war. Peter's not a crybaby, but all of us ganging up on him was too much. He got crazy upset and chucked that ice ball.

anna

I didn't want anyone to get hurt.

Danielle

Why did I go along with Jessica's plan? I could have said no. I should have said no. It was supposed to be fun. We were all getting pushed into the snow. Peter would have knocked any of us down. He's always fooling around. It was supposed to be funny. How could it turn out so bad?

Jessica

Act 8, Scene 3

I don't think any of us were malicious in our attacks on Peter.
It was the sudden onslaught that made him throw that snowball. We didn't know. And I started it.

LUKE

I was running away from Peter so I didn't actually see it. I saw something else. The *twisted* (dollar word) faces of Danielle and Anna and Jessica.

Peter

I didn't know Mr. T was going to be right there.

Danielle

Mr. Terupt stood up. Right in the way.

Jessica

I still remember Alexia's scream. Piercing. Horrified.

Peter

I didn't want to hurt anyone.

LUKE

Mr. Terupt should have stopped us. He let it go too far.

Peter

I wish I could take it back. I didn't mean to throw it.

anna

Please let my teacher be okay.

Danielle

Dear God,

It's Danielle. I really need you down here. Mr. Terupt needs you.

part two

---

march

Jessica

Act 9, Scene 1

It's been a few weeks since Mr. Terupt went into a coma. I felt numb when I first heard. My mother got a phone call on the night it happened from Mrs. Williams. The principal was calling all the parents. Mom hung up the telephone and explained his situation. I sat paralyzed, unable to move or speak. It was the second time in less than a year that I was in disbelief. The first time was when Mom told me about Dad and his girlfriend.

The day after the accident, our class had a substitute. I don't remember her name. I only remember our classroom being silent. We were given some silly worksheets to keep us busy, but no one could concentrate—not even Luke. Instead we stared blankly at the papers, or out the windows—each of us lost in an ocean of thoughts and a roller coaster of emotions. Mrs. Williams came into our classroom later that morning.

"Boys and girls, I came up here to talk to you about Mr. Terupt," she said from the front of the room. "I want you to know the truth, and not some rumor that might be floating around. Mr. Terupt is in a coma, which means he's not conscious."

That wasn't all Mrs. Williams said, but that's all I remember. I already knew the truth, but I wasn't ready to hear her or anyone else talk about it so freely. I knew about comas. People don't always wake up from them. It wasn't fair. I needed comfort. I wanted to read *Bridge to Terabithia* and *Missing May*. I wanted the company of Jesse Aarons and Summer and Uncle Ob.

Before Mrs. Williams finished, I did hear one other thing she said. She claimed that the snowball incident was an accident—not anyone's fault. I sure didn't believe that, and I know my classmates didn't believe it, either. I wondered if Mrs. Williams thought that Mr. Terupt had let things go too far. And if she did, would he be getting in trouble?

I sure hoped not. He'd been dealt enough already. Besides, Mrs. Williams was the one who gave us special permission to go outside. We could blame her. But I didn't want to see anyone get in trouble. I just wanted Mr. Terupt to wake up and fix this mess.

LUKE

I wanted to go and see Mr. Terupt. My mom and dad didn't think it was a good idea, but I wouldn't listen. I didn't stop pestering them about it. I *needed* to go. Eventually they gave in.

I stepped off the hospital elevator and stared down the long hall. Mr. Terupt was in one of those rooms. Nurses moved around behind some desks. I heard some of them laughing. How could they laugh? How could they laugh when my teacher was in a coma? They grew quiet as I walked past. I felt some of them look at me and my mom, but I just kept walking until I saw his name on the door. TERUPT. Room 404 (a palindrome, just like our classroom). I stopped and took a deep breath. I felt Mom's hand on my shoulder. I walked in.

I saw him. On his back. Perfectly still in his bed. Tubes poked into his arms. A mask covered his face. Machines beeped. His eyes stayed closed. He didn't move. Not an inch. Only his chest rose up, then fell down, with each frail breath.

I wanted to say something. I wanted to tell Mr. Terupt I was there. I wanted to tell him he was going to be okay. I wanted to, but I couldn't. I tried. I tried, and I felt a lump in my throat begin to choke me.

I didn't want to cry. I told myself not to cry. I had coached myself not to cry, but I couldn't stop it. Tears welled up in my eyes and fell down my cheeks. I turned and ran out of the room.

Mr. Terupt was going to die. I just knew it. I saw him. I saw what he looked like. He was going to die. My teacher was going to die.

The elevator doors opened and I stepped in, my mom right behind me. How could he have let this happen? Why did he put so much trust in us? He should have learned from my plant concoction. He knew it probably wasn't a good idea, but he let me do it anyway. Just like he knew our rough play outside probably wasn't a good idea, but he let it go again. He should have yelled at us. He should have yelled at Peter for the Frisbee. He should have yelled at him for the puddle of water. He should have yelled so that we knew he was serious—then this never would have happened. He should have stopped us. Now he was going to die.

We stepped off the elevator and walked to our car. As we pulled away, I saw the word HOSPITAL written on a sign. Mr. Terupt slept in the *hospital* (dollar word). I almost smiled.

Jeffrey

Terupt's in a coma. I know what that's all about. I remember from when I was little. Comas are terrifying. I'm never goin' back to a hospital. Those places are full of bad memories and bad luck. I'd like to see Terupt, but I can't visit him. I can't do it. Luke told me it was scary. I know. People in comas die.

It shoulda been me in that coma . . . not Michael.

It should be me in that coma . . . not Terupt. Peter's snowball shoulda hit me. Now our teacher's gonna die. This sucks. School sucks. Everything sucks. It was better when I didn't care.

anna

I heard Luke telling Jeffrey that he went to see Mr. Terupt in the hospital—that it was awful, and that Mr. Terupt wasn't awake or moving. But I couldn't help feeling the way I did. I wanted to go and see him, too. I just didn't think I could do it alone. So I asked Jessica and Danielle to go with me.

We sat at lunch. We were quiet. No one talked much—not since the accident.

"Anna, what's wrong?" Jessica asked. She's always good at knowing when something's not right.

"Nothing," I said. I pulled my PB&J apart.

"Just tell us," Danielle said.

I still didn't say anything. I focused on my sandwich—picking at it but not eating.

"Come on," Danielle urged.

I blurted it out. "I want to go and see him." Silence. I brushed my sandwich pieces into a pile. I noticed Danielle and Jessica weren't eating, either. The three of us busied ourselves with staring at our food.

"Me too," Jessica finally said.

"Really?" Danielle said. "Aren't you guys scared to go?"

"Yes," I said. I skooched forward. "So let's go together. Will you guys go with me?"

"I will," Jessica said, pushing her food aside.

"You think your parents will let you?" Danielle asked.

She was asking both of us, but I answered. "I already asked my mom. She said she'd take us."

"I'll try," Danielle said. "I want to go."

"We're stronger when we stick together. Remember?" Jessica said. "Just like Mr. Terupt told us."

Her voice got quiet as she mentioned his name. We got quiet. We didn't talk about him anymore. It hurt too much.

Danielle

I knew Mom and Grandma would have a fit about me going to the hospital with Anna—especially with her mother—but I didn't care, not this time. I found the courage to ask them because it was important to me.

We were sitting in the kitchen preparing dinner. I peeled the potatoes. Grandma peeled the apples for one of her delicious pies. Mom managed everything else. "When do you think this snow's gonna be gone?" Grandma asked. Farmers love to talk weather. A nice hot apple pie did sound wonderful in this cold, snowy weather. I inhaled deeply and then took the plunge.

"I want to go and see my teacher," I said. "Anna's mother is driving her and Jessica. I'd like to go with them."

"You're not going anywhere with that girl and her mother. We've already told you that," Grandma snapped.

"Mother," Mom said, "I'll handle this. Keep an eye on dinner. Danielle, come with me."

"I don't like it," Grandma said. Apple peels missed the pile and flew onto the floor.

I'm so grateful my mom pulled me away. I love Grandma, but she's like a piece of iron. Unbendable. And forget about the teacher thing. In her mind, a teacher's still the person that raps you on the knuckles with a ruler, or across the backside with a paddle. She doesn't get Mr. Terupt at all. According to Grandma, this whole incident was his own fault.

"Seems to me that teacher of yours has only himself to blame," Grandma said one night while doing dishes. "If he had more control over them boys, specially that Peter, this wouldn't have happened." I stopped drying the plate in my hands. "He needed a lickin' months ago. And a good teacher woulda given him one." My plate smashed onto the kitchen floor. I didn't mean to drop it.

Mom, on the other hand—she gets it. I've told her about Mr. Terupt many times, so I know she understands how special he is. We sat on my bed, side by side—not looking at each other, but at the wall across from us. I'd hung my sketch of Mr. Terupt there.

"You really think you want to see him?" Mom asked.

"Yes."

"It's not going to be easy. He's going to have machines and tubes hooked up to him. He's not going to look at you or say anything."

"I know. Luke was talking in school about his visit. He said it was scary."

"And I don't like you being around Anna, or her mother, but I also think it's probably better that you go with your friends than alone."

"Charlie could drop me off and pick me up." The bed bounced as I twisted to face Mom. It sounded like she was about to agree. "Please."

anna

It was time for us to go to the hospital. Jessica and her mother were already at my house. Our moms sat in the kitchen drinking coffee, like they often do now. Jessica and I sat around with some books, but even she found it difficult to focus enough to read.

"Danielle's here," I announced as soon as I saw the pickup truck pull into our snowy driveway. Mom came to the porch door to greet her with me.

"Oh my goodness," I heard Mom say to herself. She didn't even realize I was staring right at her. "Same old red farm truck." Did she know that truck? I didn't get it.

"Hi, Danielle," I said as Danielle came up the steps. "This is my mom, Terri."

"Hi, Danielle," Mom said. "Come on in out of the cold."

Danielle stomped the snow off her shoes on our welcome mat. I took her coat and hung it on our rack. "It's nice to finally meet you. Anna has told me so much about you," Mom said. They shook hands.

"It's nice to meet you, too, ma'am," Danielle said back. "Thank you for letting me come with you."

"I'm glad you could join us," Mom said. "And you can call me Terri."

I led Danielle farther into our house. When I looked back, Mom stood gazing out the door. After a few long seconds she turned away. She smiled at me and said, "Why don't you give Danielle a quick tour of the house and hang out for a few minutes, then we'll go."

"What were you looking at?" I asked.

"Nothing, really."

"That's my brother, Charlie, who dropped me off," Danielle said.

"I didn't know you had a brother," I said.

"Yeah, he's twenty-seven. A lot older than me. He works on the farm with my dad and grandpa."

I looked at Mom. She's twenty-seven, too.

"He drives that red Ford everywhere," Danielle said.

"Always has," Mom said. "Does it still have a dent in the driver's-side door?"

"Yes, ma'am," Danielle said.

My jaw dropped. What was going on? How did Mom know that? And why wasn't Danielle as shocked as me about her knowing? I looked at Mom, but before I could get anything out of my mouth (I didn't know what to say, anyway), she said, "A quick tour, Anna."

Danielle

You're young—just like my brother, I wanted to say to Anna's mother—but I didn't want to be disrespectful. So I didn't say anything as she stood staring out the door at Charlie. I could tell Anna was playing matchmaker again, but I didn't say anything about that, either. My family would never want to see Charlie and Terri together. Never.

I also met Jessica's mom. She was very nice. "You can call me Julie or Ms. Writeman—whichever you're more comfortable saying," she said.

Anna's house was simple, but nice. I guess you didn't need a big old house when it was only you and your mom. The thing I liked best about Anna's place was the artwork hanging on some of the walls. I took a closer look at one sketch and read the name, Terri Adams, at the bottom.

Anna's mother was an artist? I looked down at the sketch I held in my hands, the one that came from my bedroom wall. I had brought it to leave in Mr. Terupt's room. Ms. Adams must have noticed me looking at her work and my work.

"Is that one of your sketches?" she asked. "Anna has told me that you're a beautiful artist." I held the drawing out for her to see, but I didn't say anything. "Well, I'd say Anna was right. That is a lovely piece, Danielle."

"Thank you, ma'am," I said.

"You've done some wonderful things with shadowing and texture." She pointed to different areas of my sketch.

"I'm not sure what that means, ma'am, but thank you."

"Next time you come over, I'd be happy to do some sketching with you," she said. "And I'll give you a few pointers, if you'd like."

Next time I come over, she had said.

Anna and Jessica and her mom joined us. "Told you she was an amazing sketch artist," Anna said to her mom.

Ms. Adams smiled at us.

"Come on, Danielle. I'll show you some of Mom's other drawings and my bedroom."

I followed Anna, but not before I returned Ms. Adams's smile. I wondered what could possibly be the bad influence in Anna's house. I liked it here. And I liked the two people who lived here. I also knew Grandma wouldn't be as easily convinced.

After hanging out in Anna's bedroom, it was time to go. On the car ride, the three of us sat in the backseat: Jessica held her book, Anna held her plant, and I held my special sketch. We were all quiet. I stared out the window at the passing snowbanks and tried to keep from thinking about the snowball day, but that was impossible. For the rest of my life, I knew that snow would trigger my memory of the accident.

Jessica

Act 9, Scene 2

> **Characters:**
> **Me,** *me*
> **Julie,** *my mother*
> **Danielle,** *my friend*
> **Anna,** *my friend*
> **Terri,** *Anna's mother*

Action.
The elevator doors opened. We stepped into the white hall.

I thought of my first day at school, when my heart had thumped in my chest. The smell of disinfectant had lingered in the hallway. The smell of rubbing alcohol and iodine dominated this hospital hallway. Instead of the chatter of schoolkids arriving after a summer vacation, the only thing I could hear was the incessant beeping of those scary machines. This was way worse than the first day of school. I swallowed.

I gripped and squeezed and fidgeted with the book in my hands, *Al Capone Does My Shirts*. On that first day, Mr. Terupt had told me that he liked happy endings, so I brought him this book. I knew that he wouldn't be able to see or read it, but I wanted him to have it. Plus, having something in my hands helped me with my nerves.

I'm glad his door wasn't too far away, otherwise I might not have made it. But I did. And so did Danielle and Anna. We were there for each other.

We stopped just outside his door. The black marker spelled out TERUPT. I rubbed my finger on it. It didn't smear. I looked at Danielle and Anna. There was no hiding our fear. My mother and Terri stood behind us for support, but they also let us do this on our own. I looked back at them.

"We're right here," Mom said.

"We'll come in with you," Terri added.

I took a deep breath and readied myself for what I would see.

anna

"How're you doing?" Mom asked.

I shook my head. The hallway was so sad and frightening, and long. Beeping and coughing and moaning noises came from everywhere. Mom placed her hand on my shoulder. "I'm here," she said.

"How did you know about the dent in Charlie's truck?" I whispered. I couldn't stop thinking about it.

"I'll tell you later."

"Do you know him?"

"Yes, I know Charlie," Mom said, "but I had no idea he had a little sister."

We stopped. Mr. Terupt's door was cracked open, but not enough for me to see inside. Suddenly my worries and questions about Mom and Charlie vanished. They were quickly replaced by all my worries for Mr. Terupt. Was I ready for this? Danielle, Jessica, and I looked at each other and did our best to prepare for what was coming next.

Danielle

There was no turning back.

Dear God,
   It's Danielle. Please be with me. I'm going to need your help.

I guess I could have waited in the car, or in the lounge, but being with brave friends kept me moving forward.

Beep . . . beep. Cough. Cough. Hack. Hack. Hack. Moan . . . moan . . . groan.

The chorus of hospital noises made me cringe. I felt my shoulders pushing into my ears. We walked past an old lady sitting in the hallway. She was shaking and drooling in her wheelchair. I could hear Grandma saying, "You better put me in the ground before you send me off to one of them places with all those droolin' geezers." For a second, I laughed inside, thinking of that, but just for a second.

We stopped. The sign on the door said TERUPT. The door was partially open, but I couldn't see inside. That's probably a good thing, because I may have run back to the car had I seen what Mr. Terupt looked like. The three of us nodded at each other silently. We were ready. Or so we thought.

This is when I'll need you most.

Jessica

Act 9, Scene 3

Action.

Mr. Terupt's door stood slightly ajar, so I slowly pushed it open and stepped into his room. He wasn't alone, but he didn't have a roommate. He had a visitor: Alexia.

I stopped. Danielle and Anna saw her, too. We all stopped. Alexia was by Mr. Terupt's bed, her back to us. She didn't know we were there. I could hear her talking to him.

"Like, I've been trying to be nice, Teach. I've been quiet. I don't know, like, what else to do. I haven't been mean. You'd be happy about that, Teach. I've been doing it your way. But, like, I still need your help. I need you to come back. Everyone needs you back."

I stood right beside Alexia now, but she remained unaware. She buried her face in Mr. Terupt's bed and sobbed. I looked at my teacher. He rested peacefully in his white bed-sheets amid tubes going in and out of his body, and screens with green numbers and lines on them, and beeping noises. I felt him telling me what to do.

I reached out and placed my hand on Alexia's back.

She lifted her head and looked at me through her tear-filled eyes. I started crying then, too. Alexia stood up and we hugged. A big hug.

"I'm so sorry," she said.

I felt her squeeze me tight. "Me too," I said.

"I've never been to California," she blubbered. "My mom threw my dad out of the house last year. He never got sick."

Alexia sobbed into my shoulder. I squeezed her tight now. Through choked tears I said, "My dad's not around, either. He's still in California with his girlfriend."

We held the hug. Not with lazy arms, but strong arms. We squeezed all our sorries out in that hug. When we let go, Alexia hugged Danielle and Anna just the same. Tears filled all our eyes now, even my mom's and Terri's.

We sat in chairs next to Mr. Terupt's bed. We sat on both sides and said nothing. I placed my book on the stand next to his bed. Anna put her plant by the window, and Danielle tacked her sketch to a wall. We thought our own thoughts and stared at our teacher, who lay motionless with his eyes closed. Yet somehow I felt better. The power of Mr. Terupt, even in his coma, made something huge transpire. I felt light,

Alexia

There was no way I could like, stay away forever—especially after hearing Luke say he'd been to the hospital.

I didn't have a dad to take me, and my mom was waiting tables from noon to closing time every day of the week now. That made it easy for me 'cause there wasn't anyone at home to say "Where do you think you're going?" or "You aren't going anywhere," but I was still scared.

I made my mind up and like, rode my bike there one day after school. I knew what room he was in 'cause I heard Luke say it. When I got there, I went straight to the elevator and up to his floor.

"Can I help you, honey?" one of the nurses asked as I hurried down the hall.

I didn't look at her. I just shook my head and kept going until I found the room. I walked in.

My hands flew to my mouth. I knew Teach couldn't move, but like, I hadn't expected him to be hooked up to so many tubes. I stood frozen for a long time. Slowly I found the courage to tiptoe closer to his bed.

"Hi, Teach," I said. "It's Lexie." Already I fought back tears. "I'm sorry. I'm so sorry. I shouldn't have been mean to you. I wanted to hate you for saying those things to me, but you were right, Teach."

I knelt next to his bed and pulled his blanket in my fists. Then the big tears came. Raindrop tears. They poured from me. I couldn't help it. I cried like I used to when Mom and Dad would fight. I sobbed for a few minutes before I wiped my face on his covers. Teach just looked like he was sleeping. Was he really going to die?

"Like, I'm doing better now, Teach. I'm not being mean. You'd be happy."

I squeezed his blanket in my fists again and clenched my jaw to fight back more raindrop tears.

"Teach, like, there's something else I need to tell ya. I'm not sure but I think I saw Peter leaving here. Like, he's the one who threw the snowball, Teach. I know he didn't mean it. He didn't want this to happen. He loves you. All of us do." I dabbed my eyes with his blanket. I cried more now, but I kept talking to him. "Peter hasn't, like, said anything in school. He hasn't talked to anyone. Not a word. But no one's trying to talk to him, either. He did throw the snowball, even if he didn't mean for it to hit you. So it's still his fault." I felt bad for Peter. Everything was such a mess, and I had so many mixed-up feelings.

I had my face in his blankets when I felt the tap on my shoulder. I looked up and Jessica was there, and so were Danielle and Anna. I hugged them. I told them I was sorry. And then it was over. All of a sudden I had three friends. Like, Teach helped me, even in his coma. I missed him so much. He had to wake up. I had never felt so happy and sad at the same time before.

anna

Charlie is Danielle's twenty-seven-year-old single brother. He's the one who dropped Danielle off at my house, and he's the one who arrived to pick her up after our hospital trip. He didn't get out of his red truck and come to our door because he didn't need to—Danielle was ready. Next time I'll keep her busy so he has to ring our doorbell.

"Thanks for taking me tonight, ma'am," Danielle said as we stood on the porch.

"You're welcome over anytime, Danielle," Mom said. "I'd love it if we could draw together." Danielle smiled at that idea.

"See you tomorrow," I said. We hugged.

"Thanks," she whispered.

We watched her walk out to the farm truck with the

dented door. I held my breath with hope for the entire long, long minute. Then I was rewarded. Charlie turned his head and looked back. I saw his smile and friendly wave, a wave that Mom gladly returned. I walked to my bedroom and sat on my bed, suddenly exhausted. Mom sat next to me.

"Quite an afternoon, huh?" she said.

"Yes," I said. "Poor Alexia. No dad for her, either."

"Everybody's got a story, Anna."

I lay down and rested my head on my pillow. Mom lay down next to me. "Is Mr. Terupt going to be okay?" I asked.

"I don't know, honey," Mom said. "I sure hope so." She wrapped her arm around me and I started to cry.

"Is it my fault?" I asked.

Mom sat up. "Is what your fault?"

"Mr. Terupt lying in that bed."

"Anna, how could it possibly be your fault?" Mom sounded shocked.

"Because I'm one of the kids who got Peter mad enough to throw that snowball."

"Anna, you listen to me." She sounded almost mad now. "Look at me." Her eyes narrowed on mine. "You didn't throw that snowball, nor did you force Peter to throw it. I'm not sure whose fault it is that this happened, or if it even matters, but I do know it's not yours. Do you understand me?"

"I just want him to be okay."

"I know, honey. Me too."

I never thought I'd have the courage to ask my mom the next thing that came out of my mouth, but my feelings just poured out after seeing Mr. Terupt like that. "Do you ever blame me for what happened to you all those years ago?"

"Blame you?"

"Is it my fault that you were ostracized?"

"Anna, honey, please tell me you're not being serious."

I didn't say anything.

"My goodness." Mom placed her hands on my cheeks and spoke softly. "Anna, I consider myself lucky to have you. I would endure all that pain again in an instant so that I could have you. I've never blamed you, nor will I. You're everything to me." A tear fell from Mom's face and landed on mine. "I've always been afraid that you'd end up hating me for bringing you into this situation," Mom said.

"You're the best mom ever," I said. "I love you."

"I love you, too." Mom bent forward and we hugged. Then she kissed me on the cheek and lay back down next to me. I wanted to ask her about Charlie, but I was wiped out, so I closed my eyes.

Danielle

I'm glad I went to see Mr. Terupt. It wasn't easy, but it would have been a lot harder alone. I don't know how Lexie did it. But I'm glad she was there, because now we're friends again. I don't think she'll be mean anymore. I think Mr. Terupt helped her. Right from his coma, he helped the four of us make wrongs right.

I didn't know about Jessica's father. She seemed so perfect—I thought her family was, too. I used to think Lexie was so lucky as well. Maybe I'm the lucky one, even with this extra meat on my bones. Maybe we're all lucky for having Mr. Terupt.

I've been trying to figure out why the accident happened. Every night I pray and ask for help making sense of the tragedy.

Mr. Terupt helped Lexie and us, and he helped me make it over to Anna's house. I want to go again. Her mom's very nice. And, when he picked me up, I noticed that Charlie seemed to like looking at her. I decided not to say anything, though—not to Charlie, or about wanting to go over to Anna's again. Not yet.

At home, Mom and Grandma asked me how my visit went as soon as I walked into the kitchen. "Did that woman do or say anything crazy?" Grandma wanted to know.

"Was she okay?" Mom asked gently.

"She seemed fine," Charlie said. He came to my rescue and then walked out of the room.

"She was friendly. And I liked her," I said. "Can we just pray together for Mr. Terupt? It's late and I'm tired."

"Sure, sweetie," Mom said. I could tell that Grandma didn't like this one bit, but she went along with it.

In school the next day, Jeffrey asked a lot of questions about our visit. He had asked Luke questions, too.

"How many tubes did they have hooked up to him? What was the name of the stuff they were putting into him? Were they giving him blood? What was his heart rate?"

"Jeffrey, stop," I said. "We don't know the answers and your questions are upsetting me."

"Sorry," he said.

"You should just go yourself."

I saw him exchange a look with Jessica. I got the feeling that there was something I didn't know.

"Sorry," he said again. Then he walked away.

Dear God,

It's Danielle. Things down here are getting harder. I'm doing my best, but it's not that easy. Thanks for returning Alexia, a brand-new Lexie. I'm very grateful for that, but I'm about to ask for more.

It's Mr. Terupt. He really needs you. He looked terrible when I saw him. There are so many of us down here that want him back so badly. He's the best teacher any of us have ever had, and I just know he's got lots of good left to do here. Comfort him if he hurts, and please heal him.

There's Jeffrey, too. I saw the look he gave Jessica. Something is up with him. Please help him. And I'd like to pray for Jessica and Lexie and Anna—all three of them without dads. That's just another reason why we need Mr. Terupt back.

And last of all, I want to pray for me. I'd like to go over to Anna's house again. Maybe you can help me with that? I've also been thinking a lot about who's to blame for Mr. Terupt's accident. I thought it was Peter, because he threw the snowball. But after seeing Mr. Terupt, I'm wondering if it was me. I'm the one who suggested going outside, and I helped push Peter down. So I don't think I'm completely innocent. Please forgive me. Amen.

LUKE

I didn't think it would be as difficult going to see Mr. Terupt the second time. I knew what to expect. I was wrong.

Seeing Mr. Terupt in that bed again wasn't any easier. I thought he would look better. I thought he was improving. But he looked the same. Still just lying there in his bed. Surrounded by the same beeps and tubes and monitors and noises from the hall. It was all just the same.

I felt the lump in my throat growing. Mom's hand touched my shoulder. She saw it happening, too. I stood at the side of my teacher's bed in a state of disbelief, feeling helpless.

Then the doctor walked in. At least I figured he was the doctor. He had salt-and-pepper hair, a white coat, and a smart face. He nodded to us and then moved toward Mr.

Terupt. He checked some numbers and fluids, pulled back Mr. Terupt's eyelids to look at his pupils with his penlight, and then started to leave.

"Wait," I said. "Wait."

He stopped and turned around.

"Are you Mr. Terupt's doctor?" I asked.

"Yes. I'm Dr. Wilkins. One of the physicians."

"Is Mr. Terupt going to get better?"

I saw him take a big breath. He looked at my mother first, then me. "I don't know, son."

"What's wrong with him? He's in a coma, but what's wrong with him?"

Dr. Wilkins pulled some chairs over for all of us to sit in. He sat across from me.

"Mr. Terupt did a lot of wrestling while growing up, and even into college," he started to explain. "It turns out he had to give it up because he suffered multiple concussions along the way. These concussions have weakened his brain in certain regions. The snowball that was thrown hit one of these weaker areas—the *temporal* [dollar word] region, to be exact—and it cracked his skull." Dr. Wilkins looked very sorry as he said this. I don't know if he expected questions, but I had them.

"Does that mean Mr. Terupt wouldn't be in a coma if he hadn't suffered the multiple concussions?" I asked.

"I can't say for sure, but probably not."

"What do you do now? Just wait?"

Dr. Wilkins took another big breath. I got the sense there was more to the equation. More bad news, or news he was hoping not to share. He glanced at my mother, who nodded, giving him the okay to explain. I didn't want a sugarcoated report. I wanted the facts, and my mom knew that.

"Mr. Terupt has some bleeding going on behind this crack, and blood is *collecting* [dollar word] in his brain. We hoped it would stop, but it hasn't. He'll need to undergo brain surgery so that we can clamp the bleeding vessels."

"And then he'll be okay?"

"If it works—hopefully, yes."

I heard the word *if* loud and clear. "And *if* it doesn't?" I said.

"Brain surgery is risky. There's always a chance the patient won't recover."

"You mean die," I said. Mom put her arm around me.

"What's your name, son?"

"Luke."

"Yes, Luke. Your teacher could die during or as a result of the surgery. But I'm going to do my very best not to let that happen."

I got up and stood by Mr. Terupt's bed. I looked at him.

Dr. Wilkins got up and stood next to me. "He's a pretty special teacher, isn't he?" the doc said.

I could only nod. Speaking would have made me cry like a baby.

"I'll do my best, Luke. That much I can promise." He squeezed my shoulder and left the room.

Brain surgery, I thought. Mr. Terupt might never come back.

I ran out into the hall. "Dr. Wilkins!" I yelled. He turned around. "Does anyone else in my class know what you told me?"

Dr. Wilkins walked back toward me. "We didn't know anything about his concussions at first," he said, "but another teacher, Ms. Newberry, was able to provide us with Mr. Terupt's background information. I guess Mr. Terupt had told her about his wrestling days, and it's a good thing, because we have no other contact person for him."

I stood there quiet. No other person . . . there was nobody for Mr. Terupt.

"But to answer your question, there is another student in your class who knows what I told you," Dr. Wilkins said.

"Who?"

"I think he said his name was Peter."

I was silent. Peter? I didn't think Peter had been here. Dr. Wilkins turned to leave. "Wait," I said. "Does Peter know about the concussions, or just that brain surgery is next?"

"Just about the brain surgery. Why do you ask?"

"Because Peter threw the snowball."

april

Jessica

Act 10, Scene 1

Mrs. Williams assumed responsibilities as our teacher. She recognized and acknowledged our *huge* mess, and that our feelings—despite our being just fifth graders—were very real. I respected Mrs. Williams for her courageous act, but it didn't change a thing. Mr. Terupt still lay motionless inside the vast whiteness and beeping of that building. Our classroom remained as lifeless as our teacher. We needed Mr. Terupt back.

Things happen for a reason. That's what I told Jeffrey. Did I believe that? Sometimes. What were the reasons for my dad leaving us? I haven't figured that out yet. And what are the reasons for Mr. Terupt's predicament? I've decided they're different for everyone, and maybe not there at all for others. I see the reason for Alexia now. Without this accident, I'm not sure she would have made it back as my friend. Without this accident, I bet Danielle never would have made it over to Anna's house. But what about someone like Luke or Jeffrey? I don't see any reason for either one of them. And I can't find any reason for me.

LUKE

The classroom persisted in *secreting* (dollar word) *unbroken* (dollar word) quietness. I stayed quiet, too, even though I had a lot bottled up inside me about Mr. Terupt's brain surgery. Peter knew about it, but he didn't have all the details. I know he blames himself. You can see it. Ever since the accident, he walks around like a mummy. He *should* be blaming himself. He threw the snowball. But if it had hit anyone other than Mr. Terupt, I don't think we'd be experiencing a tragedy like this. That's what Peter needs to know. It doesn't make everything all better, but it might help ease his pain.

I can't tell him, though. No one is talking to him. But that's not why I don't want to talk to him. I don't want to find out *why* he threw that snowball.

Danielle

It was springtime. I sat on the front porch with Grandma after church. She drank her coffee (black, because she's tough) and I sipped some iced tea (unsweetened, because I hope to be tough like her). I love these moments with Grandma.

"There's nothin' like a New England spring, Danielle," she said. "You endure the harsh winter, and because of that you learn how to really appreciate the new season."

I knew what she was talking about. The snow had melted and the birds had flown back, singing and praising. Flowers popped up and buds appeared. The animals on the farm acted frisky. Time to rejoice. But I couldn't, and Grandma noticed.

"I'll bet you in other parts of this country, where there's

no real winter, people miss out on spring," Grandma said. "That's just a shame."

I nodded. This spring was different, though. My teacher still slept, and this weighed on me and sucked the happiness out of everything. I felt like I was still in my winter slumber.

"Danielle, let's pray." I bowed my head and closed my eyes. I figured Grandma was going to thank our God for the beautiful weather and the gift of spring. That would have been fine, but she took me by surprise.

"*Dear God, Mr. Terupt needs you. Now, I don't understand teachers these days, but I've come to realize that this Mr. Terupt is as good as they come. I've seen how he has touched my grand-daughter and her friends. He's special. You don't need him up there yet. So you make sure you give him back to us real soon. Amen.*"

Grandma had understood the important stuff. Her prayer made me feel better. I always feel better with Grandma on my side, even when she's telling God what to do.

"Thank you, Grandma," I said. "I love you."

"I love you, sweetie. I'll keep praying for him."

I stayed in my winter slumber even after Grandma's prayer. But then, unexpectedly, I startled awake. Not because of encouraging signs from Mr. Terupt, but because of Anna's shocking news.

anna

I pumped my legs back and forth on the swings. I needed to get some momentum going so that I wasn't just sitting with my feet dangling in the puddle below me. Danielle, Jessica, and Lexie sat on swings, too—Danielle right next to me. It was nice to be outside for recess again, now that the snow was gone.

"Charlie was at my house when I got home from school yesterday," I said. Danielle's pumping stopped. "Mom told me they were just sharing a cup of coffee and some conversation." Danielle pumped slowly again, but she still didn't say anything. "If Charlie marries my mom, what would that make us?" I went on. "Sisters!"

Danielle put her feet down and hopped off her swing. She

turned to face me. My pumping slowed. Was something wrong? She looked right at me.

"Anna, Charlie will never marry your mother," Danielle said. "My family would never allow it."

I stopped my swing. Jessica and Lexie stopped theirs, too. "Why?" I asked.

"My family . . . ," Danielle started to say, then her chin and voice lowered. "My family doesn't approve of your mother."

I felt like I'd just got run over by Charlie's red truck. My whole body grew weak. "But my mom's a good person," I said.

"I know," Danielle said. She scuffed the mud with her foot. "But it's not that easy. If it weren't for Mr. Terupt's accident, I don't think I would have ever been allowed to go over to your house."

I learned something that day. Even after all this time, my mom was still ostracized for something that happened long ago. And because I had contributed to Mr. Terupt's accident, I was going to pay for it the rest of my life.

Jessica

Act 10, Scene 2

I discovered another reason for Mr. Terupt's predicament the day Anna and Danielle and I were on the swings—a reason bigger than simply getting Danielle over to Anna's house. That was only a start. Just like Mr. Terupt had helped Lexie reunite with Anna, Danielle, and me, I had to wonder if maybe Mr. Terupt's accident was going to help Danielle's family accept Anna and her mother. I hoped so.

Jeffrey

Boring day after boring day puttered by. Life was back to normal, where everything sucked. We all thought about the same thing, but never talked about it—not everybody together. Little groups whispered here and there, but that was it. I didn't participate. Too many bad, scary memories. Then somethin' happened to break the silence.

Jessica

Act 10, Scene 3

Enter Miss Kelsey.

"I came up here today to share some news with all of you," she said, a smile on her face. How could she smile at us like that? Didn't she know? "James is going to be leaving school."

More sad news, I thought. Great.

"This is wonderful for James. He's been doing so well in school—he now has a chance to join a classroom like yours, in the town where he lives."

We stayed quiet. I knew I was supposed to be happy for James, but I didn't feel excited about anything right now. I think everyone felt the same way. Miss Kelsey started to look puzzled. She didn't understand our silence, but Mrs. Williams gave her an encouraging nod.

"The Collaborative Classroom would like to invite all of you to a surprise going-away party for James," Miss Kelsey went on. "You've invited us to so much, and done so much for us, that we decided it was our turn to invite you to something. Plus, James loves you. You guys really made the difference. You're the reason he's improved and gets to move on."

We made the difference. I felt good for a second, but then I thought about how none of this would have happened if it weren't for Mr. Terupt. I couldn't feel happy about anything. Not without my teacher.

Jeffrey

Miss Kelsey brought us good news, and it fired me up.

"James is leaving," she said.

How was that supposed to be good news? Everybody I ended up likin' I ended up losing. Why did I even bother tryin'?

LUKE

We made our way down to the Collaborative Classroom. It was James's surprise going-away party. I wanted to be happy for him, but it was so difficult.

Terrible/Worrisome News (Mr. Terupt) + Happy Party (James) ≠ Happy Luke

Invasive species are organisms that are introduced into a new environment. Since they have no natural predators there, they thrive. They suck up all the resources, leaving nothing for the organisms that were there first. The native species suffer and die. Going down to the Collaborative Classroom, I was afraid that our whole class would act as the invasive species, sucking up all the happiness with our sour attitudes. Lucky for us, the antidote was present at the party.

The lights clicked on. *"Surprise!"* we yelled when James walked in. His face beamed. I automatically smiled, too. And then it happened.

James walked over to Peter and gave him a hug that *shattered* (dollar word) his shield. Everybody stopped and watched. This was the first time any of us had really looked at Peter since the accident. We had each made the choice to make him invisible. But now we saw him.

James finally let go and stepped back. He looked into Peter's eyes.

"Peter, not your fault. Not your fault." James's voice rose. "Peter!" Now he yelled. "Not your fault! Accident! Accident!"

The room was dead quiet, holding its breath. Peter began crying, softly at first, but then he lost it. His entire body shook with each sob.

I couldn't be a silent onlooker any longer. I stepped forward.

"James is right, Peter," I said. "It's not all your fault."

I told everyone about Mr. Terupt's early concussions, and the bleeding, and the looming surgery.

"Besides," I said, "Peter threw the snowball because of me."

I cried now, too. Accepting responsibility can make you do that, I guess. I hugged Peter. Right there on the spot. I walked over and hugged my Elmer's sneakers nemesis.

And then our crying classmates hugged us.

Thank you, James.

Alexia

Like, isn't it weird that Peter called them retards way back when Teach first told us that we were going to work with them? And then it was like, one of the "retards" that helped save Peter. We're lucky some people are so full of goodness.

Like Jessica and Anna and Danielle. I was mean to them, but now they're my friends again. I'm lucky. I was lonely without them.

I bet Peter was lonely, too. But like, none of us did anything about it until James said something. Then I felt bad for Peter. I gave him a hug. He didn't deserve to be all alone.

It feels good being nice. I like it better than being the old Lexie. I hope Teach gets to see how he helped me.

Jeffrey

Things happen for a reason. Jessica told me that.

I didn't hate Peter. Even if I wasn't smilin' on the outside, he had me laughin' on the inside a lot. He just liked to have fun, and the good fun went real bad on him that day in the snow. That's all. It wasn't all his fault. James told us that. James had more courage, more good heart in him than any of us "smart" kids.

I don't know if James's words alone woulda been enough, but then Cool Man Luke came to the rescue. Not just Peter's rescue, but all our rescues. We needed to talk. Thanks to James and Luke, we started to.

Things happen for a reason. I can't find all the reasons. Did everything we did with the Collaborative Classroom lead toward this moment? Is this why it all happened? Why did it have to be Peter? And why did it have to be our teacher in a coma? Was it so that I would learn that life isn't fair sometimes? 'Cause I learned that a long time ago with Michael.

ANNA

Things are working out, sort of. There's been good news for James, Lexie's back to being nice, and Peter's part of our class again. But it's hard to stay positive when Mr. Terupt is about to have brain surgery. I get scared when I think about it for too long, and I think about it all the time—that and my mom.

Danielle's words crushed me. I didn't get mad at her, though. In a way, I felt sorry for her. I know she wants to be my friend, but her family doesn't want that to happen. That's got to be hard. This time I talked to Mom about it as soon as I got home that day.

"Mom, Danielle said her family disapproves of you, and that you and Charlie will never be allowed to get married."

"Whoa! Slow down, Anna," Mom said. "First of all, Charlie and I aren't looking to get married. Second of all, I know their family disapproves of me." My jaw fell open. "Sit down, honey."

I sat at the kitchen table across from Mom. She had been looking over the mail and drinking a cup of coffee (cream and sugar) when I burst in on her.

Mom explained. "Charlie and I went to school together. When I ended up pregnant with you, he didn't treat me kindly—just like everyone else. In fact, one day he got me so upset I kicked his truck. I put that dent in his door." I could see my mom reliving those painful memories as she spoke. "He's actually apologized to me for how he behaved back then."

"But why would Charlie say he's sorry if his family disapproves of you?" I asked.

"Danielle's parents and grandparents are pretty old-fashioned and religious. Just like my parents, who couldn't find a way to be accepting of me and my situation all those years ago. They still can't."

For a second I wondered about my mother's mom and dad. I've never met them. Were they really that unforgiving? Were Danielle's?

"I think Charlie just went along with everyone else when we were teenagers, but now he's ready to think for himself. It's always good to make up your own mind," Mom said.

So I have Mr. Terupt to thank. If it weren't for his accident, Danielle might never have come over, just like she said. Thanks, Mr. Terupt, but you didn't need to go and get hurt this bad so that I could be friends with Danielle. Don't get me wrong—I'm very grateful—but I'd really like you back now. You're going to get better. *Be positive*. You taught me that.

"Maybe Danielle and Charlie will be able to change their family's opinion of us," I said. "I'm going to be positive. Mr. Terupt would want that."

Danielle

I know what it's like to have people gang up on you. Being big, I learned real quick. It stinks. I never thought I'd do that to someone else, but I did. I didn't even realize it.

Peter must have felt that no one in the whole wide world liked him. I see it now but I didn't see it when it was happening, when it mattered most. Not until James and Luke made me open my eyes.

Selfishness caused me to be blind. I only thought about how bad *I* felt. I'm not saying I would have done anything different, had I seen it earlier. I'm just glad it changed. For all of us.

Luke told us that Mr. Terupt's going to have brain surgery. All the girls started crying when he told us that. And the boys didn't make fun of us for it—not like every other time. Luke kept talking. He told us about Mr. Terupt's wrestling and concussions and it not being all Peter's fault. It was an accident, a real honest accident, with lots of us to blame. Luke said that Peter threw the snowball because of him. But he wasn't the only one who got Peter mad that day. Others of us started confessing. I prayed for God to cleanse us all.

I hugged everybody at James's party. I was sorry for so much, but really sorry for Peter. Even though we all told him it wasn't just his fault, I think he still felt it was.

I felt bad for Anna, too. I hoped she wasn't mad at me after what I had told her. I wanted us to still be friends. I also wondered what Charlie's intentions were toward her mother, so I asked him.

I found Charlie out in the barn early one morning before school. He was sitting next to one of the cows and pulling her teat to get her started for milking. "Morning, sunshine," he said. "What brings you out here?"

"I wanted to know why you went to see Terri Adams," I said.

"To share a good cup of coffee with a fine woman," he said, "and to ask for her forgiveness for the way I treated her when we were in school."

Charlie slipped the machine onto the cow's udders and got her milking. "Good girl," he said, patting the cow. Then he walked over to the next one, squatted down, and started the process over.

"Do you think Anna and her mom are bad influences on me?" I asked.

"Nope. But I don't think you should try to change Grandma's or Mom's opinions on that score."

"Are you going to see Terri again?"

"I'd like to," Charlie said. He stood and moved to the next cow. Charlie had four machines, so he could milk four cows at the same time. He did the milking every morning and night.

"Then are *you* going to try and change their opinions?"

"Nope. I see no reason to start a family war—you shouldn't, either," he said.

"That's easy for you to say, because you can just drive yourself over there whenever you want. Sooner or later my teacher won't be in the hospital any longer. He'll either be back or in the ground, and I won't have any reason to go over to Anna's house. I want to be friends with her and her mother. I like them."

Charlie stopped what he was doing and looked at me. "Let's cross that bridge when we come to it," he said. "And let's continue to pray for that teacher of yours."

"Do you think he'll make it through the surgery?"

"I don't know," Charlie said. "I wish I could tell you, but I only know animals." He walked over to me and wrapped his arm around me, giving me a little squeeze. "It's time for you to catch the bus. Go on. Have a good day at school, sunshine." He made me smile a little. I hoped I didn't smell too much like the barn.

Jeffrey

If anyone knows silence, it's me. The silence in our classroom wasn't the worst. There was always someone you could
turn to and whisper. It contained tons of sadness and guilt,
but it wasn't absolute.

Even Peter's silence was over. He was lucky.

My silence at home pressed on—with nobody for me to
turn to, and with nobody in sight to rescue me. That silence
was absolute. The only company in my house was more sadness and guilt.

But somewhere along the way this year, Terupt taught me
to see things different. To think about things different. To
think about more than just me. It was always *my* silence, and
my fault. But now I started to think about Mom's silence.

And Dad's silence. Mom's fault. And Dad's fault. They were hurting, too. Why did I have to wait for them to talk to me? I didn't.

A few days after James's party I crept into Mom's bedroom, where she lay on the bed in her pajamas. I climbed in next to her and put my arm around her. Then I told her, "It's not your fault. I love you." She didn't do anything, but I lay there and fell asleep, holding my mom.

When I woke up, I felt good. I hoped my words had helped her. I thought of Terupt as I walked out of her bedroom. He had helped me reach out. I missed him. I wished I had a chance to tell him how I felt, too. I wanted him back so bad.

I found Dad sitting in a chair in the family room—better called the "be-alone room" in our house. He was home, so I must have slept for a while. I wondered if he had seen me with Mom. Immediately, I knew it was gonna be much harder for me to say those same words to him. We never talked to each other like that, not even before Michael died.

"Hi, Dad." I sat on the sofa near his chair.

"I saw you in there with your mother," he said. "She needs you, Jeffrey. You might be the only one who can help her."

"Dad, it's not your fault," I blurted out. He didn't say anything. I knew my words surprised him. That they hit hard. I got up and went over and hugged him. "I love you," I said. I let go after a few seconds and headed out of the room.

"It's not your fault, either," Dad said, before I was gone. I heard his voice breaking up as he said it. I felt that good feeling again, and thought of Terupt.

I thought about what my dad said about Mom needing me. I didn't know what else to do, so every day after school, I started going home and resting next to her in bed. It felt like the right thing to do.

I *tried*. Terupt taught me that, too.

may

Jessica

Act 11, Scene 1

Welcome to the hospital waiting room, where every face is a concerned face. Who knows what's on the minds of all these worried people? They keep busy in different ways. Some read, a few watch television, one lady knits.

Enter us. The kids from room 202.

We sat quietly, kind of looking around—anxiously awaiting the outcome of Mr. Terupt's surgery. Was it even okay to talk? I wondered. A lot of other people from school sat waiting, hoping for Mr. Terupt. Mrs. Williams and her red-haired secretary, Mrs. Barton, waited. Mr. Lumas and Mr. Ruddy sat and waited. Everyone at school liked Mr. Terupt. That was just another testament to him.

Technically today was a school day, but Mrs. Williams helped us make arrangements to be here.

"I can't make this a school-sponsored field trip," she told us about a week ago. At that point we knew when Mr. Terupt's surgery had been scheduled, and Mrs. Williams realized our entire class planned to be there. "I can't have all of you climb onto a bus and be taken to the hospital," she said.

"Our parents can drive us there," Anna suggested. "And we can help each other with rides."

"I like that idea," Mrs. Williams said. "Then you can leave when you want, or not go at all—if you'd rather not." I thought about Jeffrey.

Ms. Newberry, Miss Kelsey, and Mrs. Warner also came. The school was able to provide substitutes for their classes, but not everyone's. I expect all the teachers would have been here if it weren't a school day.

That was when I realized that Mr. Terupt didn't have any family present. Not one person. I thought of his desk back in our classroom. Every teacher has family pictures on his or her desk. Not Mr. Terupt. And there were only two flower arrangements in his hospital room, one from Ms. Newberry and one from Snow Hill School. But no mom or dad were sitting next to his bed. How had I missed it? Not one family picture. Not one family member visiting or waiting next to me. Did he even have any family? I wondered. Had my mother noticed and not said anything? Had any of my classmates had these same thoughts? All of a sudden there was so much I didn't know about my beloved teacher.

"I just wish he'd open up more and give me a chance," I heard Ms. Newberry say. She was talking quietly to Mrs.

Williams. "He was beginning to let me get close. I don't know what he's so afraid of."

"Or what he's hiding," Mrs. Williams added.

"I just want the chance," Ms. Newberry said. "I care about him so much, and so do these kids. He better pull through."

I heard Ms. Newberry's voice crack. Mrs. Williams put an arm around her. They were quiet. I suddenly had a lot of unanswered questions going through my mind, but none of them mattered if Mr. Terupt didn't make it through the surgery.

"How long will his operation take?" Anna asked.

She didn't realize she had blurted this out until she met our startled looks. Thanks, Anna, I thought. The perfect candidate to break our silence.

"Eight hours," Luke said. "Less, if it goes well—more, if there are any complications."

Silence again.

LUKE

I'd visited the hospital several times, but never once had I gone to the waiting room. Not until I sat in there with my class on Brain Surgery Day. Sat for hours.

The room had a nice layout. The architects had found a way to *maximize* (dollar word) the area while keeping a large perimeter. The room represented a rectangle, with little sections of the wall jutting into the interior here and there. This created corners and smaller spaces within the larger room. I figured this was important because people wanted privacy. At least, that was how it felt while I waited.

Danielle

We sat together in the waiting room. I sat next to my mother. We left Grandma home, not knowing how she would handle being in the company of Terri and Anna. Anna sat across from us, next to her mother. A large wooden coffee table rested in the middle of everyone. It reminded me of our class meetings. We didn't form a circle on the floor, and we didn't have the microphone, but it was close enough—except no one talked. Mr. Terupt always started our meetings, so we sat silent, until Anna spoke up. Thank goodness.

But after Luke answered her question, no one else talked. At least not until Jeffrey surprised us. He put our class microphone in the middle of that big wooden table. I stared at it. Then I looked at Jeffrey. How did he know to bring it?

"Just a hunch," he said. I noticed that he and Jessica were looking at each other.

I reached down and took the microphone. "Remember the first time Mr. Terupt brought this out?" I said. I passed the microphone to Lexie.

"I was like, Teach is a weirdo," she said. "But it turned out to be pretty cool. Sort of like the grass thing."

"Seventy-seven million, five hundred thirty-seven thousand, four hundred twelve," Luke reminded us. "That grass project was awesome."

The microphone moved around our square, and we shared different stories and memories. It was perfect.

Then a doctor came into the waiting room.

Jessica

Act 11, Scene 2

Enter a man wearing lime green scrubs and a matching hospital cap. The kind that cinches around your head like a shower cap. I saw him the moment he came through the door. Was he coming for us? It was too soon! Wasn't it? Had something gone wrong with Mr. Terupt's surgery? I stiffened. Then I noticed Jeffrey. He was practically hyperventilating. This place, and especially the sight of a doctor, triggered such horrible memories for him. I wrapped my arm around him and whispered, "It's okay. Just breathe." My mom also helped comfort him. She sat on the other side of Jeffrey and hugged him, too. Mom knew his story—I had told her. But others stared at him, wondering why he was so worked up.

The doctor didn't come over to us, and Jeffrey calmed

down. Instead the doctor made his way over to the knitting lady. I saw him take a deep breath as he got closer to her, and I wondered if it was one of those big breaths you take in order to get ready to deliver bad news. He pulled a chair next to the knitting lady and sat down across from her.

Once she realized he was there, her hands and yarn and needles all stopped working and rested in her lap. Her eyes looked into the doctor's face.

His lips never moved, but his head shook from side to side and his face expressed sorrow.

The knitting lady's strong chin dropped. The yarn and needles fell to the ground, and her hands covered her face. She began to shake silently with lonesome tears.

The doctor placed a hand on her back. He said, "I'm very sorry." He waited for a while, then rose and walked out of the room.

I felt silent tears trickling down my cheeks. I looked at my friends and saw some of them with tears, too. I was scared, but I wasn't alone.

Jeffrey

Hard to breathe. So many bad memories. Bad news everywhere. I saw the doc walk in. I couldn't catch my breath. Jessica noticed. She and her mom wrapped their arms around me and helped me calm down.

The doc wasn't for us. He handed out his bad news to someone else. I know how that goes.

"I'm so sorry," the doc had told my family. That was all he had to say. We knew Michael was dead.

Danielle

Peter took the microphone. He still wasn't talking. He'd answer you if you asked him something, and we weren't ignoring him anymore, but for the most part he stayed silent. And he never talked about Mr. Terupt or anything to do with the accident. I held my breath along with everyone else—at least, that was what it felt like.

"I remember the time I said we should invite the Collaborative kids to our holiday centers. I saw Mr. T wipe his eyes after I said that. I didn't know why then. Now I do."

Peter put the microphone back on the table.

Alexia

I took the mike again after hearing Peter. Like, I knew what he was talking about, understanding stuff about Teach that he didn't before. That was true for me, too.

"Teach took me in the hall and, like . . . said some stuff that I hated him for. Really hated him. But all he did was tell me the truth. I didn't want to listen. I hated him and the truth."

I stopped talking, but I didn't pass the mike yet. I was thinking.

"I hope Teach wakes up so he can see that I've listened," I added. "He helped me. I'd like him to know that."

I put the microphone back on the table. Peter picked it up again.

Peter

I decided to pick up the microphone again and say one more thing. Maybe talking about Mr. T and sharing memories would help him pull through the surgery.

Surgery. Brain surgery. I couldn't believe he had to have brain surgery. And all because of me. Because of the snowball I threw. My thoughts always came back to this.

"I remember the time I flung that Frisbee. Mr. T said a few things to me, but that was it. I remember the puddle on the floor. He said a few things, but that was it. Nothing bad ever happens, I thought. I chucked that snowball. No matter what any of you say, it's all my fault. It always will be." I stopped talking so that I could fight back my tears, but I didn't put down the microphone. I wasn't done yet.

"I'm sorry," I said as I looked around at everyone. "I'm sorry you're here because of me." I let the microphone roll back onto the table.

No one had time to respond, because another doctor walked in—and this time, he was our man.

Jessica

Act 11, Scene 3

The door to the waiting room pushed open and another doctor walked in. Same lime green scrubs and matching cap. This doctor also wore a mask tied around his face.

Jeffrey started hyperventilating again. Mom and I calmed him. We held hands on Jeffrey's lap. I squeezed Mom's hand and she squeezed back. Was this it?

The doctor reached behind his head and untied the mask. He was our guy. I saw him take *that* deep breath as he walked toward us.

LUKE

I saw Dr. Wilkins approach us. My heart took off like a car that had its gas pedal mashed to the floor. Please, please, please have good news! I repeated over and over again in my head. Mom squeezed my shoulder.

Dr. Wilkins found a chair and sat with us. "Good news, gang," he said. "Mr. Terupt made it through the surgery."

Our faces broke into mini-smiles and we let out breaths of relief. I gave Mom a little hug.

"We were able to stop the bleeding, but your teacher remains in a coma," Dr. Wilkins continued.

"Why?" Anna said. "I thought that if you stopped the bleeding, he'd wake up." Her voice rose and shook a little. "I thought that was what's supposed to happen."

Anna spoke for all of us. But instead of Dr. Wilkins answering, Jeffrey did.

"Now it's wait and see," Jeffrey said. He took a deep breath in and let it out slow. "That the bleeding stopped is a good sign"—deep breath—"but that doesn't guarantee Terupt will wake up. We have to wait and see." More deep, slow breathing. Why was he so anxious? His difficulties made me realize that he hadn't visited the hospital, but always seemed interested in my report. What was Jeffrey's deal?

"That's right. We wait and see and keep hoping," Dr. Wilkins said.

"Can we see him?" Peter asked.

"Not today, Peter. Mr. Terupt is in a postsurgical room being watched carefully."

"Why does he need to be watched carefully?" Anna asked, her voice barely a whisper. "I thought he was okay now."

"We monitor every patient closely after a major surgery. It's normal," Dr. Wilkins promised. "Mr. Terupt is doing well at this point."

We sat there looking at him like a team that had just lost their big game.

"Hey, guys—don't give up now," Dr. Wilkins said. "This is when your teacher needs you most. This is good news today."

And then Anna came through in the clutch. She took the lead and said what we needed to hear. "He's going to make it. *Trust me on this one. Be positive.* Mr. Terupt told me that once, and he was right."

Jeffrey

It was "wait and see" for Michael, too. He didn't make it. That was when Mom and Dad's lives suddenly crashed down different paths. I don't know if their paths will ever come together again, but it's okay to hope. I hope Terupt makes it. I'm tryin' hard to believe Anna.

Jessica

Act 11, Scene 4

That was it. Wait and see. It felt so anticlimactic—to sit all day expecting an outcome, only to find that it was time to go home and wait some more.

People trickled out of the waiting room at different times. Some of the adults left first, probably because they're more accustomed to being patient. Miss Kelsey and Mrs. Warner left, then some of my classmates. Only a few people were still sitting—Anna and Terri, and Danielle and her mother—when Mom and I rallied ourselves to leave. Lexie and Jeffrey came with us. We were their ride home.

Wait and see.

ANNA

The waiting room slowly emptied. Next thing I knew, my mom and I were sitting directly across from Danielle and her mother with hardly anyone else around. I felt uneasy, knowing her mother hated us, but I took a chance.

"Danielle, can we pray with you?" I asked.

Danielle didn't hesitate one second. "Sure," she said.

We bowed our heads and Danielle led us in a prayer for Mr. Terupt. It was a beautiful prayer, and afterward I thought her mother's eyes looked differently upon me.

Mom and I left after that, leaving Danielle and her mother, Luke and his mother, Peter, Mrs. Williams, and Ms. Newberry. How close were Mr. Terupt and Ms. Newberry, both without wedding rings? I didn't know, but my heart suddenly hurt for the teacher from across the hall. She was definitely hoping to have him back. You didn't even need to be good at noticing things to see that. So many of us need you, Mr. Terupt. Keep fighting.

Danielle

"Can we pray with you?" Anna asked me. I felt alarm rush through my mom's body. How could these sinners want to pray with us? Mom must have wondered.

"Sure," I said.

"Dear God, we're down here playing the wait-and-see game now. It'd be great if you could keep the waiting part short, and give us back Mr. Terupt. There are lots of people hoping he wakes up. Please give us the strength to keep hoping and believing as we go on waiting. And God"—I whispered this last part, because Peter was sitting near us—*"I also ask that you give extra comfort to Peter, and Jeffrey, too, though I'm not sure what's up with him. Amen."*

Anna's smart. She wants our families to get along, so she

asked to pray together, knowing that God is most important to my family. I know my mom can't think Terri's all bad if she's praying with us, and Anna is as nice and sweet as she is. At least I hope that's true. I've been asking God to help me get my family to see that Terri and Anna are good people.

Jessica

Act 11, Scene 5

We dropped Lexie off first, then Jeffrey. I sat in the front passenger seat and Jeffrey sat in the back. Before he got out, I asked him, "You okay, Jeffrey?"

"Yeah, I'm okay," he said. "Thanks for helpin' me in there. Thanks, Ms. Writeman."

"You're welcome," we said together.

"I'm sure everybody's wonderin' what's up with me," he said.

"Don't worry. Your secret is still safe," I said.

Jeffrey opened the back door, but he didn't get out right away. "There's something I've been meaning to tell you, Jess. What happened to Terupt isn't your fault. You need to stop thinking that it is."

Jeffrey's words startled me. I did feel guilty. I'd roped Danielle and Anna into my wicked plan, which led to Peter's devastating snowball. "Then why did it happen, Jeffrey?" I said. "I told you things happen for a reason, and I still don't know mine."

"Neither do I," he said. "But not knowing the reason doesn't make it your fault."

We sat quietly. Mom didn't say anything. I stared down at my hands. They longed for a book to hold. I fidgeted with my nails and cuticles instead. Then Jeffrey spoke again.

"I know one thing, Jess." He had called me Jess twice now. "You've helped me. I haven't had someone to talk to in a long time. Thanks." He climbed out of our car and shut the door. Before driving away, we saw Jeffrey's mom standing at the front door to his house, waiting for him—and she wasn't wearing pajamas. They hugged.

Mom and I had tears in our eyes as we drove away. More of Mr. Terupt at work, I just knew it. We hadn't driven very far before Mom broke the silence.

"Jessica, I need to tell you some things that even adults have a hard time understanding, but I need you to try, okay?"

I nodded and sat up straight in my seat to readjust my seat belt.

"I know you've been wrestling with the issue of whose fault Mr. Terupt's accident is, as have many of your classmates. Poor Peter's really struggling, and I'm afraid the only one that might help him is Mr. Terupt." Mom slowed to the stop sign and looked both ways.

"So whose fault is it?" I asked, my voice rising. Emotion

can do that to you. Mom just went with the flow. She turned the car left and stepped on the accelerator.

"Mr. Terupt's," she said. I looked out my window. I didn't want to hear it. "Look, Jessica, you don't have to agree with me, and not everyone will, but you need to hear me out. Let me explain." Slowly, reluctantly, I looked at her. I didn't want her to be right. "Thank you," she said. "I told you it wasn't going to be easy." We slowed at a red light.

"All those instances with Peter earlier on this year, and with Luke's plant concoction, and all the other mischief." Mom paused. "I think Mr. Terupt handled them the way he did because he was trying to teach you guys some personal responsibility." The light turned and Mom pushed the gas. "But that's what cost him in the end. He let you play rough that day in the snow and hoped you wouldn't cross the line— but he made it *your* responsibility not to cross that line because he didn't intervene."

"But how is that bad? Isn't that one of the reasons he was so special, because he gave us those chances?"

"Don't use the past tense, honey. He is special."

"Fine," I said, annoyed, but glad to talk about him in the present. "But isn't it?" I was annoyed because I didn't want the conversation slowed. I wanted answers. I cracked my window, suddenly hot. I let the wind hit me in my face.

"It is indeed one of the reasons he's special. But in the end, you're still just kids, and asking you to assume that much responsibility isn't fair. You can't be expected to handle it all the time. So that's why it's his fault." Mom spoke so calmly. I knew she was trying to keep me from getting too upset.

"It's his fault for asking us to act like adults when we're just kids," I said, restating Mom's argument. "Whereas, if he had taken the responsibility out of our hands by making us stop playing rough, then there probably never would have been a snowball thrown." I looked at Mom.

"That's right, exactly," she said.

"Well, I think that makes about as much sense as Dad and his airheaded bimbo." Our car swerved. Mom was in shock. We hadn't spoken about Dad in a while, but he and his stupid girlfriend boiled to the surface of my upset feelings. Plus, I have a strong vocabulary and could have probably selected a nicer word for her, though I doubt I could have chosen a more accurate one. "So now if Mr. Terupt gets better, he's going to get in trouble. Is that right, too?"

"Not necessarily," Mom said. "And watch your language. Besides, to say airheaded and bimbo is a bit redundant, though I'll agree, the new woman in your dad's life is a real floozy." The car slowed and Mom pulled into our driveway. She put the car in park and turned it off. I undid my seat belt. "Jessica, I've spoken to Mrs. Williams and to some of the other parents and adults at school on several different occasions. We've been talking because we're worried about how you're all dealing with this. Nobody wants to see Mr. Terupt get in trouble, including Mrs. Williams and the school. Everyone knows he's a great teacher. We all just want him to get better."

Mom leaned over and gave me a hug. I hugged her back.

"You know, Terri told me the other day that Anna asked her if their situation is her fault."

"Anna's fault?" I said. "Of course it isn't."

"Exactly," Mom said. "And I hope you know what happened between your father and me is not at all your fault, either."

I needed to hear that. I hugged her again, but I didn't say anything because talking would have made me cry. And Mom was quiet, too—I think for the same reason. Quiet love filled our car.

june

Jessica

Final act, Scene 1

Welcome to the last day of school, where there's music and movies and games, singing and laughing and smiles all around, cakes and cookies and fun for everyone. At least, this is what the last day of school is supposed to encompass. Ours didn't. Crying wasn't anything I had ever experienced on any last day of school, but crying was what I felt like doing, and I know I wasn't the only one. We had held tremendous hope for our teacher to be with us by the end of the school year— but he wasn't.

I keep wondering about the Mr. Terupt I don't know. I've thought a lot about it since that day in the waiting room. Everyone likes Mr. Terupt, but nobody is that close to him, except for Ms. Newberry. But even she hopes to get closer.

Part of me thinks that it's not just him they're all concerned about, but us, too—because they know we're the ones who are *really* close to him. But how can I even say that, or think that, when I don't truly know him? Maybe it's because it doesn't matter how well we know him. We love him.

I haven't talked to anyone else about this, not even my mom. I want to, but what's the point—he's not here. Mr. Terupt didn't make it.

Alexia

I went to see Teach last week and like, the nurses said they were doing something and that I had to come back. I was mad, but I didn't really think anything was up.

Now I'm beginning to wonder if maybe something's going on. Mrs. Williams and Ms. Newberry are definitely acting strange. Like, Mrs. Williams is way too perky—humming to herself and talking with silent nods to Ms. Newberry, who's been poking her head into our room one too many times today. I'm beginning to wonder if Teach woke up. And like, they've been keeping it a secret so that they can surprise us. I'm telling ya, something's up.

Danielle

Dear God,

 I don't want to be mad at you, but I am. You haven't listened to my prayers. If you had, Mr. Terupt would be here. We need him. Why didn't you give him back to us?

anna

Mrs. Williams makes me mad. Our whole class is feeling terrible, except for her. She seems happy—walking around with that bounce in her step. I even heard her humming at one point, but she quickly stopped when she realized I had noticed. Is she really that happy to get this year over with? Then the thought hit me: Does she know something that we don't?

LUKE

No Mr. Terupt. Suddenly things changed drastically for me. I'd kept believing that he was badly hurt and would recover, but now that the year is over, the thought of him not making it seems very real. I'm scared.

Jeffrey

I don't know what's going on with Mrs. Williams, but I want to punch her. This is the worst day of the year, and I see her wink at Anna. "What's the matter with you?" I want to scream at her. I don't care if she's the principal. "In case you didn't notice, Terupt's gonna die!" I want to yell that at her, too. But I keep all my anger inside. Don't you dare wink at me, lady.

Jessica

Final act, Scene 2

All day long I fought back tears, and now tears streamed down my face. I couldn't believe it. Mr. Terupt made it. He was here. He was okay.

We rushed out of our seats. Our bodies pressed together in a giant class hug.

"I missed you," he said.

"We missed you, too," we shouted.

"I love you guys," he said, bending down to our level. He looked at each one of us and hugged us one by one. He hugged me.

"I love you, Mr. Terupt," I said. The words danced out of my mouth.

"I love you, too, Jessica."

We hugged some more, and then Mr. Terupt spotted Peter. Peter hadn't been part of the hug. He was still sitting in his seat—probably too scared to move, too frightened to think what Mr. Terupt might do or say to him.

Mr. Terupt stood up and walked over to Peter. We watched, and he taught us like he did every day we were with him. He showed us how to forgive.

LUKE

Mrs. Williams spoke up. "Boys and girls. I do have one announcement before I leave you with your teacher." She smiled. "The school board has decided that next year will be an experimental year. We're going to try looping in one classroom."

"What's that?" Anna asked.

"Looping is when a class and the teacher move on to the next grade together," Mrs. Williams said.

It got quiet fast. Real quiet. Hold-your-breath quiet. Was everybody wondering the same thing? I looked around. Jessica smiled and nodded at me.

"Boys and girls, next year *your* class will be looping," Mrs. Williams said.

"With Mr. Terupt?" Anna asked.

"Yes," Mr. Terupt answered.

We jumped and screamed and hooted and hollered. I saw Mrs. Williams heading toward the door. I ran over to her.

"Mrs. Williams," I said as she was about to leave.

She turned around. "Yes, Luke?"

"Thank you," I said. Then I felt a sudden quietness behind me. The rest of my class stopped and took notice of Mrs. Williams.

"Thank you, Mrs. Williams," voices called.

She looked at Mr. Terupt. I was close enough to hear her say, "There's magic in this room with you here, Mr. Terupt. Magic." She hugged him and left.

Alexia

Teach made it. He like, showed up on the last day with no warning. It was the biggest surprise ever. Everyone ran over and hugged him. Then Teach went over and hugged Peter.

I liked Teach so much when he did that. It made me think of the day he took me out in the hall. Teach knew how to be nice. He didn't, like, say one thing and do another. Not Teach. After things calmed down, I went up to him.

"I've, like, been being nice now, Teach," I said. "You'd be proud."

"You've always been nice, Lex," he said. "You've just figured out how to show it. But you're right, I'm very proud of you."

"I can't wait till next year," I said.

"I can't wait, either. I missed you."

Then I hugged Teach again. "I love you, Teach," I said.

"I love you, too."

So now it's like, wait till next year. And I can't.

Jeffrey

Sometimes school can actually be great—and next year's gonna be just that, 'cause Terupt's back.

I didn't think he was gonna make it. I thought he was gonna die, like Michael did. I tried to help Michael and it didn't work. I don't know if I helped Terupt at all, but he made it. I ran and got help when he fell down in the snow. I ran inside and got the nurse and made them call 911 and got Mrs. Williams. I did that. Was that enough?

I watched Terupt hug Peter. He didn't blame anyone. Jessica told me that it wasn't my fault that Michael died. Maybe you just do the best you can, 'cause you can't control what happens in the end. I guess it's okay to hope for things. Sometimes it works out.

Slowly, I'm getting my mom and dad back. There isn't

silence between us anymore, though they still don't talk to each other very much. Mom is out of her pajamas, but never out of the house. That's okay for now. She's starting to try to get better, like me and Dad. I hope things get better between them.

I miss my brother but I'm real glad we got Terupt back. And I think I've found some reason for all of this. I never woulda been the one to break the silence between me and Mom, and me and Dad, if it weren't for Terupt's accident. I wanted so bad to tell him how much I loved him, and I didn't know if I was gonna get the chance when he was in that coma. And that was when I knew I didn't want to miss the chance with my parents, so I broke the silence. I'm glad, too. I'm happy.

anna

The last day turned out to be a great day. Mr. Terupt made it! I've never felt so happy. My throat, my heart, my belly— they all burned with happiness, and probably relief, too. And then we found out about this looping thing, and I felt the good hurt inside all over again.

"Bus nine. Bus nine is now loading," the call came over the speakers.

"See you soon, Mr. Terupt," I said. I ran over and gave him another quick hug. "Have a good summer."

"You too, Anna," he said.

"And Mr. Terupt." I looked up at him and he looked down at me. "I think Ms. Newberry might have the hots for you, in case you're interested." I smiled.

He smiled back. "Matchmaker Anna. Thanks for the tip."

"Bus nine. Last call for bus nine," the loudspeaker announced.

I hurried out of room 202 with my head held high. I never made it to bus 9, though. I got downstairs to the lobby and ran into Mom and Charlie.

"Hey, kiddo," Charlie said.

"Hi, guys," I said. "Are you here to pick up Danielle, too? She's still upstairs." I barely got those words out of my mouth before I saw the answer to my question. Danielle's mother walked into the lobby. She spotted us right away. "Hi, Mrs. Roberts," I said, finding no small amount of courage. "Would you like me to go upstairs and get Danielle for you?"

Not needed. Danielle came through the stairwell door and entered the lobby. She took a second to look at everyone. Then she and I exchanged a knowing glance, bracing ourselves for whatever came next.

There would be no disappointments on this day. It was a day of happiness and celebration. "Hi, Mrs. Roberts," Mom said, offering her hand to shake. "I'm Terri Adams, and this is my daughter, Anna. We didn't meet properly at the hospital. We'd love to have you and Danielle come over this afternoon. Maybe for a cup of coffee or tea, and some hangout time for the girls."

The ball lay in Mrs. Roberts's court now. I let my breath out when I saw her shake my mom's hand. "Please, call me Susan," she said. "Danielle and I would be happy to come over." She glanced at Danielle, who nodded excitedly, but without hiding the shock on her face. Then Mrs. Roberts looked at Charlie.

Mr. Terupt came into the lobby at some point during all this and gave Danielle and me a thumbs-up sign. It was as if he knew the whole story. Did he?

We waved good-bye to the best teacher in the whole wide world.

Danielle

It started with an old friend (Alexia), who wasn't really a friend. In came this new girl (Jessica), whom I liked but was told not to like. Somewhere in between I became friends with Anna. We worked with the Collaborative Classroom and had this huge Ramadan project. And that old friend, who I had figured out wasn't a friend at all, was kind of on her own. I had Jessica and Anna.

Then the accident happened. While Jeffrey ran for help, I held Mr. Terupt's head, putting my hat and coat under it so that it wasn't lying on the cold snow. I went to visit Mr. Terupt in the hospital with Jessica and Anna, and found an old friend there. Alexia was Lexie again, except new and improved. James left, but he made us see Peter again. And then we played the wait-and-see game until today.

Today Mr. Terupt came back! And then we found out that we're looping and will get to be with him again next year. I can't wait to tell Grandma the news. She's the one who helped me when things got tough, and she said a lot of prayers for us. I don't think I'll tell Grandma about the end-of-the-day news, though. I'll leave that up to Mom.

I'd just wished Anna a great summer and watched her head out of the classroom to catch her bus when Mr. Terupt said, "Danielle, I see your mother walking across the parking lot." He was looking out our window. "She must be here to pick you up."

"Okay. Thanks," I said. I grabbed my stuff. "Have a great summer. I can't wait for the fall."

"Bye, Danielle," he said.

I ran over and hugged him once more. "I'm so glad you're back," I told him. I let go, looked in his face, then hurried downstairs.

I got down to the lobby and saw everyone—Mom, Charlie, Anna, and Terri. Was Charlie with Mom or Terri? Oh boy, I thought. But things worked out. Mom shook Terri's hand and accepted her invitation for coffee. Mom looked at Charlie after, but didn't say anything or make any sort of face. She was going to try really hard for us.

As we were leaving, Mr. Terupt gave us a thumbs-up sign. How long had he been watching? How much did he know?

Dear God,

It's Danielle down here, full of love. Thanks for giving me my teacher back, and again for next year. And thanks for helping my mom give Terri and Anna a chance. Maybe now you can start to work on Grandma—she's going to be a lot tougher to persuade. Amen.

P.S. I'm sorry I got mad at you.

Peter

Out of nowhere, I heard the screams. "Mr. Terupt!" Everyone around me jumped up and ran toward the door. I couldn't believe it. Mr. T was back.

I started crying. Mr. T was alive. And he was here. I stayed in my seat, trying to look small. But he spotted me. The room grew quiet as Mr. T walked toward me. I was scared again.

Mr. T got down on his knees and looked directly into my eyes. Then came the best hug I've ever felt. Mr. T wrapped his arms around me and gave me a huge squeeze. I squeezed him back as tight as I could. My body shook and I sniffed my snotty nose.

"It's okay, Peter," he whispered in my ear. "I forgive you."

Suddenly I felt lighter. A lot lighter.

Jessica

Final act, **Final scene**

I've realized something. It's not California I long for anymore, or even Dad—it's sixth grade and another year with Mr. Terupt. I want to ask him about his family, and tell him to let Ms. Newberry get close because she truly cares about him, but now isn't the time. There will be lots of opportunity for that when school starts up again. I need to enjoy this curtain call.

I've read a lot of books, but I think ours is a great story, and I know Mr. Terupt would agree. It's a happy ending.

LUKE

I remember thinking, sixth grade. We're going to be sixth graders. And Mr. Terupt is going to be my teacher. Our teacher. I thought of Mrs. Williams's word, *magic*. I looked at Mr. Terupt sitting with some of my classmates. And I thought, she's right, there will be magic.

He's my teacher. The Dollar-Word Man.

Terupt *(dollar word)*

ACKNOWLEDGMENTS

I want to express my heartfelt thanks to the following people:

To an inspiring and fun group of women: Meg, Thea, Martha, Betsy, Debbie, and Leigh Ann, who first listened to the voices in *Because of Mr. Terupt* and who gave me the courage to keep going.

To John Irving, truly one of the most generous people I've ever met. Your encouragement and wisdom have given me something I can never repay. I am forever grateful.

To Paul Fedorko for stepping in and helping my novel find a home.

To my editor, Françoise Bui, for her patience and persistence, listening, and careful work with the manuscript.

And lastly, to my wife, Beth, who encouraged and supported my pursuit of my new writing passion several years ago. Behind this good man, there is a one-of-a-kind woman.

ABOUT THE AUTHOR

ROB BUYEA taught third and fourth graders in Bethany, Connecticut, for six years before moving to Massachusetts, where he now lives with his wife and three daughters. He teaches biology and coaches wrestling at Northfield Mount Hermon School. *Because of Mr. Terupt* is his first novel.